BAR 10 JUSTICE

Gene Adams sends some of his Bar 10 cowboys to assist the law in protecting his rancher neighbours, for outlaws have been rustling vast numbers of cattle. But the rustlers are far more deadly than Adams had suspected and they kill more than half of his men and the posse, including the sheriff. Unwilling to risk any more of his cowboys, Adams secretly forces the town to make him the new sheriff. And so it is that he heads alone into the Badlands. But does he have the remotest chance of defeating his foe?

BOYD CASSIDY

BAR 10 JUSTICE

Complete and Unabridged

LINFORD
Leicester

First published in Great Britain in 2004 by
Robert Hale Limited
London

First Linford Edition
published 2005
by arrangement with
Robert Hale Limited
London

British Library CIP Data

Cassidy, Boyd
    Bar 10 justice.—Large print ed.—
Linford western library
1. Western stories
2. Large type books
I. Title
823.9'14 [F]

ISBN 1–84617–052–4

Published by
F. A. Thorpe (Publishing)
Anstey, Leicestershire

Set by Words & Graphics Ltd.
Anstey, Leicestershire
Printed and bound in Great Britain by
T. J. International Ltd., Padstow, Cornwall

This book is printed on acid-free paper

*dedicated with thanks
to the gracious Jean Styles*

Prologue

The rolling range to the north-east of the Bar 10 was one of the most fertile places in all of Texas. Most of it fell within the boundaries of Gene Lon Adams's famed million-acre longhorn cattle ranch; most, but not all.

A few hundred acres was still open range and used by neighbouring ranchers to fatten their own stock in a vain attempt to compete with Adams's legendary longhorns at the market places in McCoy and Abilene. This land of sweet grass continued up to the fast-flowing Red River which was the border with the notorious Badlands.

A place which had always been worth avoiding.

Gene Adams had lived long enough to see the land above Texas change names several times. There had been a time when it was regarded as part of the Lone Star State. For more than a decade it had been the Indian Territory, but now it was being groomed for settlers and the native Americans were once more being forced off into other less hospitable lands.

A state of turmoil had arisen from the confusion. Where once there had been several tribes of Indians living undisturbed in peace, there were now countless gangs of outlaws reining supreme in a territory bigger than most European countries.

Map-makers back East had somehow managed to get their draftsmanship wrong and had totally forgotten to incorporate all of the Indian Territory in their new proposed Oklahoma.

The resulting chaos was a safe haven for killers and cattle-rustlers alike. News spread like wildfire and soon countless outlaws found refuge in the land which on the maps of the Eastern politicians, technically did not exist.

But it did exist.

This was the Badlands.

At first the outlaw gangs kept themselves to themselves. Then they realised the fortune that lay south of the Red River. Soon riders had crossed the watery border and taken cattle off the unguarded range. Once back in the Badlands, the beef could have their brands slightly altered and could then be driven into neighbouring Arkansas or even further north to Kansas.

There was nothing any of the ranchers could do legally to get their stock back once it had entered the infamous land of outlaws.

There was no law there.

Gene Adams had never allowed his precious herds to mix with the cattle of his fellow ranchers on the open range. He ensured that his northern outpost cowboys kept all his longhorns on Bar 10 soil.

So far, the rustlers had not dared to venture on to Bar 10 land. Gene Adams thought that his own reputation would keep them at bay. For his name had taken on almost mythical proportions over the forty years that he had owned the Bar 10.

His hair had been as white as snow even back then. He had not appeared to alter at all. Always seeming neither young nor old, Gene Adams remained an enigma.

His handsome tanned features and dark eyebrows could frighten most men who dared square up to him. He simply looked like someone who could not be defeated.

And so far, he never had been.

Few had ever entered the boundaries of his vast cattle empire uninvited. Those who had, had been dealt with swiftly by Adams and his loyal riders of the Bar 10.

Gene Adams had no idea of what had occurred the previous night as he steered his chestnut mare into the wide main street of Silver Springs with his two closest friends, Tomahawk and Johnny Puma to either side of him.

He imagined that the cattle-rustling

would remain a problem for other ranchers and never concern him or his precious Bar 10.

Adams would be proved wrong.

1

One-Eyed Jake McGraw had never been a man to allow fear or respect of others to guide his actions. He had lived by one simple rule. If others had what you wanted, you took it off them by any means available. There was no emotion in the brutal outlaw except hatred.

McGraw had killed more than a score of people in his forty-three years, not including Mexicans or Indians. Women and children had also felt the cold razor-sharp steel of his deadly knife as well as the lethal lead of his guns during his relentless but vain search for sanity.

Behind the black eye-patch hid a secret which had shaped his entire adult life. One that One-Eyed Jake had never revealed to anyone.

Jacob McGraw had grown up in a

Boston asylum for the insane after killing his own parents at the age of eight. Few facts had ever become public of what exactly had occurred on that fateful day but his total lack of remorse had ensured that he had been regarded as someone who would remain within the solid walls of the 'mad house' until he himself died.

Somehow, just before his fourteenth birthday an opportunity arose which was to change everything for the strange creature who had not spoken a single word since his incarceration years earlier. Jake McGraw grabbed at the chance and managed to break out of a place from where it had long been thought impossible to escape.

Somehow, the deranged youth had managed to lay his hands on a knife in the asylum kitchen. The blood-bath that he left in his wake was so vicious that the Boston authorities were forced to offer a $10,000 reward for his capture, dead or alive.

The only part of Jacob McGraw to

remain within the dark asylum walls was his left eye. It had been clawed from its socket by a guard as he had desperately fought for his life. But the lethal kitchen knife had dispatched him along with others who stood in the way of the crazed youngster.

Nothing had been capable of stopping the frenzied McGraw as he killed his way out of the large sprawling city and made his way into the wild, mostly uncharted West.

The deadly knife would remain his only true friend for the remainder of his days. The only thing he would ever trust to do exactly what he wanted it to do. Even long after he would become an expert with both handguns and rifles, he would still favour the long-bladed knife.

It was part of him.

Driven by only one thought, McGraw knew that there was nothing that he would not do to ensure that he never returned to the Boston asylum.

He would kill anyone whom he

considered even the slightest threat to his freedom. Year after year he moved deeper into the lawless territories until he and his gang heard about Oklahoma and the strip of land known as the Badlands.

Like countless other outlaws, the troop of eight ruthless killers had aimed their mounts toward the territory. It was a place where only the most brutal had even the remotest chance of survival.

One-Eyed Jake McGraw relished every second he and his men spent in the fast-growing territory. With no law, except that of the gun, he and his men knew that they had found their own personal paradise.

His gang of outlaws were all cut from the same cloth. None had any thought for their fellow man. They were each as cold-blooded as their leader, although none of them was driven by the same madness as McGraw.

Fear of the hangman's rope was the only thing which kept them on their toes. Yet every one of them knew that they would choose death rather than capture.

Like their one-eyed leader, they would live and die with their guns in their hands.

It had not taken One-Eyed Jake long to work out that this new territory was sitting directly above the cattle-rich state of Texas. And Texas was so big it was doubtful whether it could muster enough lawmen to stop his gang from doing as they pleased. Even the Texas Rangers were sparse in the north of the vast state and McGraw knew it.

With a willing market for every head of Texan beef that he and his men could rustle, it seemed that the eight deadly outlaws had found a perfect way to make themselves rich.

Over the previous month, McGraw and his men had ridden across the Red River at its shallowest point and started to strip the fertile range of the white-faced beef cattle belonging to the ranching neighbours of Gene Adams.

They took only a few steers at first, then more and more as McGraw and his gang became better at the art of rustling.

The combined Texan herds had totalled over 1,000 and had been virtually unguarded. They had never required guarding when the Indians had been north of the border, but now everything had changed.

And not for the better.

With a million twinkling stars illuminating the lush Lone State grassland, the eight riders made their way once again into the heart of the range. The white faces of the short-horned steers stood out like lanterns in the haunting light, guiding the rustlers toward them.

This time One-Eyed Jake McGraw and his outlaws were here to try and cut out at least a hundred of the grazing steers and drive them back into the Badlands. They would get twenty dollars a head for the well-fed beasts with no questions asked.

McGraw studied the starlit range

carefully from atop his sturdy grey. The white faces of the cattle looked back at the eight horsemen with equal curiosity. There was still no one on the range to protect the well-fattened beasts.

Once more, there would be no opposition.

Perhaps the owners of these steers had not noticed that their herds were being slowly reduced in numbers, One-Eyed Jake thought to himself as he took a chunk of tobacco and placed it into his mouth.

After all, it was a very big range for ranchers to keep an exact tally of the beasts that roamed from one horizon to the other.

McGraw chewed slowly, knowing that they would find no one to stop them taking as many steers as they could find.

'C'mon!' McGraw growled to his men. 'Nice and quiet. We don't wanna spook these critters.'

The riders began to make a wide circle around the grazing cattle.

2

Gene Adams pulled back on his reins and stopped the tall mare outside the feed store. As Johnny Puma slid off his pinto pony and Tomahawk dismounted next to the long hitching-rail they noticed that Adams's attention was drawn to a group of roughly half a dozen men across the street. They ranted and raged outside the telegraph office.

'What's wrong, Gene?' the bearded Tomahawk asked as he rubbed his ancient back with his gloved fingers.

Gene Adams glanced down at his oldest friend, then returned his attention to the noisy men.

'I was just wondering what the ruckus is all about, oldtimer,' Adams replied.

'Just a couple of moaning ranchers, Gene.' Tomahawk's eyes twinkled as he

14

rested his right wrist on the gleaming metal axe head which poked from his belt. 'You know ranchers, they'll moan and groan about anything.'

Adams raised an eyebrow.

'Hold up on that gravy 'til I check the biscuits, Tomahawk.' Johnny Puma wrapped his reins around the pole, tied a firm knot, then slipped under the neck of the lathered-up black-and-white pony.

'Looks like a couple of ranchers from up north, Gene,' he observed.

Adams nodded without looking at his young friend.

'Yeah! It's Tom Smith and Morris and Carter with a few of their boys. But why are they so all-fired up?'

Before either Tomahawk or Johnny could answer, Adams pulled the head of his mare away from the hitching pole, tapped his spurs against her sides and allowed the handsome animal to walk across the wide street to where the men were still raging at one another.

'So the great Gene Adams is in

town!' Brock Carter said in a raised voice.

'What in tarnation are you boys shouting about?' Adams smiled as he looped the reins around his saddle horn and dismounted.

Each of the men on the sun-bleached boardwalk turned and looked at the familiar figure.

'This ain't none of your concern, Gene.'

Adams smiled even more broadly. He rested one of his boots on the boardwalk and pushed his black ten-gallon hat off his brow. The three ranchers who stood amid their various cattle hands were Tom Smith, Chuck Morris and Brock Carter. Unlike Adams, who had the best herd of longhorn steers in Texas, they bred white-faced cattle. All the ranchers were red in the face.

'Is that right, Chuck?' Adams went, smiling.

'Darn right!' Morris nodded firmly.

Gene Adams could hear his two Bar

10 comrades walking up behind him as he looked up at Smith and Carter.

'Look, boys,' Smith said pointing at Johnny and Tomahawk as they reached Adam's side. 'More Bar 10 vermin. Like flies around an outhouse.'

Tomahawk scratched his bearded chin and looked confused.

'Vermin? Flies? Gravy and biscuits? Ain't nobody gonna start talkin' American around here?'

'Hush up, Tomahawk.' Gene Adams grabbed his pal's jutting beard and tugged it before returning his attention to the ranchers. 'You boys are sure looking ready to burst. I ain't never been a nosy kinda man, but it seems to me that you three ain't never been the sort to have yourselves such a noisy disagreement before. Not in the middle of town, anyways. What in tarnation is wrong?'

Smith looked at Morris and then at Adams. His head lowered.

'It's them rustlers, Gene. They have been taking cattle off the range for months now and its costing us a fortune. It was just a few at first. Now the critters are taking scores at a time. Last night more than a hundred of our steers were plucked right off the range.'

'More than a hundred?' Gene Adams stepped up on to the boardwalk and rested a gloved hand on the worried rancher's shoulder.

'That was the rough tally we came up with just after dawn,' Tom Smith said.

'It must be getting mighty serious if you boys are starting to fight each other.' Adams led the men along the boardwalk in the direction of the nearest saloon. 'I reckon we ought to have ourselves a few glasses of cold beer and talk about this properly. Blaming one another ain't gonna solve this problem.'

'Have they taken any Bar 10 stock, Gene?' Brock Carter asked.

'Nope!' Adams replied. He pushed the swing-doors of the saloon open and led the anxious men into the cool interior.

'Only a madman would try and steal Bar 10 steers!' Tomahawk piped up from behind the ranchers as they all reached the long bar.

'Reckon Tomahawk is right,' Carter sighed. 'Gene here has more cowboys than the rest of us put together. No one would try and steal Bar 10 longhorns.'

Adams pulled out a few silver coins from his shirt pocket and dropped them in front of the bartender.

'Beers all round?' the bartender asked.

'Yep!' Adams nodded.

Tomahawk leaned closer to Adams and whispered:

'I could use something a tad stronger than beer, Gene. I need somethin' to ease up my roomatiz.'

'Ya lucky I'm letting you have beer, you old buzzard,' Adams said. He tugged the jutting beard again, then moved closer to the troubled ranchers.

'We need help, Gene,' Tom Smith reluctantly admitted.

'What about the sheriff?' Johnny

Puma suggested.

'The law ain't got no jurisdiction in the territories, let alone the Badlands, Johnny,' Adams said.

'How on earth did you know the rustlers are from the Badlands, Gene?' Brock Carter asked as a glass of beer was placed before him on the damp counter surface.

Gene Adams placed a gloved hand on the bar and tilted his head until his blue eyes burned into the rancher.

'It stands to reason that the rustlers are using the Badlands as a base, Brock. They could take all our cattle in there and we ain't legally got any right to get them back.'

'But we have to get them back, Gene,' Morris protested.

'Yeah.' Adams nodded.

'I'm facing ruin if we don't, Gene,' Carter added.

'We all are!' Smith sighed.

'If we can't legally go into the territories and bring our steers back, what can we do?' Morris asked.

20

Gene Adams lifted his glass to his lips and drank the cold beer thoughtfully.

'Have you boys tried asking Sheriff Doyle for some help?'

The ranchers moved around the tall Bar 10 man.

'Nope! We can't even find the old fool, Gene,' Morris grumbled. 'I don't think he's in Silver Springs.'

'He's probably high-tailed it and gone fishin',' Brock Carter added angrily. 'Whenever there's trouble, he disappears.'

Adams finished his beer and placed the empty glass down on the counter. He signalled to Johnny, then grabbed Tomahawk's collar as his drink was placed before him.

'Gene?' Tomahawk whined, his fingers just failing to grab the beer glass before he was hauled away from the bar. 'I ain't drunk my beer yet!'

Adams continued walking with Johnny at his side and Tomahawk's collar firmly gripped in his right hand.

'C'mon. Let's leave these boys and

21

try to find Doyle.'

The three men walked back into the sunshine. Gene Adams looked up and down the busy street.

'What are we doing, Gene?' Johnny asked the tall rancher.

'Helping our friends, Johnny.'

'I don't even like those varmints.'

'Me neither!' Tomahawk confirmed.

Gene Adams inhaled deeply. 'Better we help them than have them start blaming us for all their misfortunes. Right?'

The cowboys shrugged.

They knew by experience that it was pointless arguing with Gene Adams. He always got his way in the long run.

'OK. What do ya want us to do?' Johnny asked. He straightened his gunbelt until it sat neatly on his hips.

Adams pointed to both ends of the street in turn.

'I want you to go looking for the sheriff. You take that end of the street, Tomahawk, and you take the other, Johnny.'

'What are you gonna be doin'?' Tomahawk asked.

Gene Adams stepped down from the boardwalk, grabbed the saddle horn and raised his left leg until his black boot slipped into the stirrup. He glided up on top of the chestnut mare and gathered his reins together.

'I'm going to ride to the Horseshoe gambling hall.'

The bearded old man lifted his battered hat and scratched his thinning hair.

'How come?'

'Because I happen to know that Sheriff Doyle likes to play poker, old-timer.' Adams winked.

Both Bar 10 cowboys watched as the rancher turned his mount's head and rode off down the street. They waited for him to turn into a narrow side street called Black Jack Lane before looking at each other. For a few seconds their faces were expressionless. Then they both began to smile. Johnny Puma's white teeth flashed in contrast to the

23

toothless grin of the older man.

'You thirsty, Johnny?'

'Sure am!'

Tomahawk looked again up the street where the dust from Adams's horse's hoofs still hung in the dry air.

'Old Gene didn't say when he wanted us to go looking for the sheriff, did he?'

'Not that I recall, Tomahawk,' Johnny replied.

'That's what I thought.'

'So?'

'That beer's getting warm in there, Johnny.'

'Then we better go drink it fast.'

'Ya gettin' smarter all the time.' Tomahawk winked.

They both pushed the swing-doors apart and returned to the bar and their waiting beers.

3

The Horseshoe gambling hall was a large wooden structure. It had to be large to cater for all the cowboys who frequented its highly decorated interior. It was said that every way known to men of losing their money lay within its four walls. Up the wide staircase lay other ways for men to spend their money and time.

Gene Adams pulled back on his reins and got down from his horse quickly. He looped the reins around one of the hitching poles and then stepped up on to the boardwalk. For a moment, he paused. This was not the sort of place that Adams cared for, and he vainly tried to discourage his cowboys from visiting it.

But he knew that when a cowboy's sap was on the rise it was far better to turn a blind eye. There had been a time when he too had been young enough to frequent such places. He had learned many things in gambling-halls. One of which was how to play poker and win. That had been nearly four decades ago though. Twenty years before most of his Bar 10 riders had been born.

Adams glanced at his gloved hands and the right hand which he never allowed to be viewed by others. He wondered whether his disfigured fingers could still shuffle a pack of cards. He had never had any problem drawing and firing his golden Colts, but the doubt lingered.

Adams removed his left glove, tucked it into his gunbelt, then pulled the black kidskin tightly over his right hand. He flexed the disfigured fingers that lay inside it. His blue eyes studied the exterior decoration. No expense had been spared in painting the Horseshoe. It was probably the most colourful building in Silver Springs. It had to be because this was the flame that lured the moths.

Gene Adams found himself brushing the honest trail dust from his shirt and pants before entering.

He removed the black ten-gallon hat and hung it by its drawstring on the grip of one of his famed golden Colts. The smell of cheap scent fought with the stale cigar smoke throughout the interior of the huge building.

The smoke was winning.

The sound of music drew the rancher through the hall and toward a large room. Sunlight filtered through a lace drape on to a dozen or more gaming-tables. More than half of them had games in progress.

Across the hall in another equally large room, Adams spied a roulette table and other strange gaming-machines. He had no idea what they were or how they were used. Apart from poker, the tall owner of the Bar 10 ranch had little knowledge of games of chance.

Gene Adams rubbed his chin with the index finger of his right hand. He felt like a fish out of water within the strange building, and it showed. He moved his weight awkwardly from one foot to the other.

'Would you like a drink, sir?' the gentle female voice asked from behind his broad shoulders.

The voice took him by surprise. Adams turned and then looked down. The girl was no more than five feet in height and far prettier than anyone who worked in such a place had the right to be, he thought. She held a solid silver tray in her small hands. A dozen thimble-glasses filled with whiskey rested upon its gleaming surface.

'I don't think so, miss.' Adams smiled and noted the neat black dress the girl wore. It covered everything but hugged the girl's shapely figure like one of his gloves.

Again, the tall rancher was surprised by the modest attire. He had expected all the females within the Horseshoe to be showing far more flesh.

'It's free,' she piped up with a cheeky glint in her large brown eyes.

Adams smiled.

'How old are you, little 'un?'

'Sixteen,' she replied.

'Sixteen?'

'Well, I will be in the fall,' she amended.

Gene Adams leaned down until his mouth was level with her left ear. He whispered:

'Have you seen Sheriff Doyle? I need to talk with him.'

'Sure I've seen him. He's upstairs.'

'Oh.' Adams straightened up and cleared his throat as his eyes drifted to the second-floor landing. He had heard stories about what was up the stairs of this place.

'How old are you?' she asked cheekily.

'Too old, dear. Way too old,' Adams admitted coyly.

'But still young enough to blush.'

Gene Adams watched as the pretty female moved away and entered the nearest room with her tray of free drinks balanced on her delicate fingers.

She was looking over her shoulder at the embarrassed man who now felt even more out of place.

'What in tarnation is Gene Adams doin' in this place?' The loud unmistakable voice of Ben Doyle boomed out as the man came ambling down the stairs buttoning up his shirt. He was carrying a bundle under his muscular arm.

Adams cleared his throat and squared up to the red-faced sheriff.

'I'm looking for you, Ben.'

Doyle stopped and stared hard into the face of the Bar 10 rancher. He could see that there was a look of disapproval in the familiar features.

'You look like you just walked in on a preacher with his pants down, Gene.'

'Well?' Adams glanced up at the second-floor landing again and then back at the sheriff.

Doyle laughed.

'Do you reckon I was up there pleasuring myself with one of the lovely females who dwell up in the red-draped rooms, Gene?'

Adams raised a black eyebrow.

'Well, you were up there, after all, Ben. What do you think I thought when I saw you strolling down them stairs doing up your clothes?'

'Takin' a bath, Gene.' Doyle lowered his chin and tried not to laugh even louder. 'I come here twice a week to take a bath in the best washroom in Silver Springs.'

'A bath?'

The sheriff raised the bundle.

'These are my dirty clothes. Did you think that I was having me some sin?'

Gene Adams turned and strode towards the door to the street with the lawman on his heels.

'Reckon I did,' Adams managed to admit as they both reached the boardwalk and stopped in the sunlight. 'What was I meant to think?'

'But I'm as old as you are, if not a tad older, Gene.' Doyle chuckled. 'I sure wish that my body was as capable as it used to be. But nowadays I have to settle for a bath. Reckon you must be in far better condition than me if you thought I was . . . '

Gene Adams turned and faced the man, looking serious.

'Hush up, Ben. I came looking for you for a darn good reason. I want you to take a posse up to the northern range above the Bar 10 and keep a look-out for rustlers coming over the Red River from the Badlands.'

The expression on Doyle's face changed suddenly.

'They stealin' Bar 10 cattle?'

'Not yet, but they have been rustling a lot of beef off the range belonging to Tom Smith and the other ranchers up there. I want you to help them.'

'I don't get paid to chase rustlers in and out of the territories, Gene.' Doyle leaned against a wooden upright and studied the tall rancher. 'I don't think you should be troubled by them though. No rustlers would try and enter the Bar 10.'

'I want you to camp there for a couple of nights and try and catch the varmints in the act.' Adams shrugged.

Sheriff Doyle began to shake his head.

'I don't think so, Gene. Like I said, I don't get paid for that kinda work.'

Gene Adams moved closer to the lawman.

'I'll give you a hundred in gold coin and provide a few of my cowboys to back you up.'

Doyle was interested. 'You're willing to give me a hundred in golden eagles for protecting other ranchers stock? Why?'

Gene Adams drew in his belly and plucked his large black hat off his gun grip before carefully placing it on his head.

'I've been lucky and have made a lot of money over the years from breeding longhorns, Ben. The ranchers up on the range are struggling to put food in their kids' mouths and can't afford to lose any of their stock. I just want to help.'

Doyle nodded.

'How many men will you send to

help me, Gene?'

'Would six be enough?'

The lawman was thoughtful as he calculated how many deputies he might be able to enlist.

'You got a deal, Gene. I'll expect the gold coin when I get back in about four days time. You send six of your best hands to meet me and my posse at Cripple Creek. I'll give it two days and nights on the banks of the Red River. If nobody shows, I'm headin' back. OK?'

'OK, Ben.' Adams stepped down to the hitching-rail and untied the reins of his chestnut mare. 'One more thing.'

Doyle looked down at the rancher as he stepped in his stirrup and mounted the tall horse.

'What?'

'Don't mention anything about the money to the ranchers.'

'Why not, Gene?'

Gene Adams turned the mount. 'Just don't tell them. OK?'

Ben Doyle nodded and watched the rider head back towards the main street. Then he rubbed his chin. He had a posse to round up.

He returned and made his way along the boardwalk in the direction of his office. Suddenly he stopped. He felt a cold chill trace his spine. The seasoned lawman swallowed hard and then continued.

4

It was late afternoon as the half-dozen riders trailed the twisting river northward. The sun seemed to have become even more merciless as the day progressed. Its blinding rays danced on the shallow fast-moving water making it almost impossible to see anything ahead of them. But these men were not strangers to this land. They knew virtually every inch of the Bar 10 cattle ranch.

This was the shortest route to the northern outpost boundary of the million-acre longhorn spread. Beyond that lay the huge fertile range that bridged the gap between Gene Adams's Bar 10 and the lawless Oklahoma territory.

The six cowboys had headed out within an hour of Gene Adams's return from Silver Springs to the heart of his ranch.

Happy Summers led the six Bar 10 rannies along the dry sun-baked river bank towards Cripple Creek. The skilled horsemen had been given their orders and plenty of ammunition by Gene Adams and told to meet up with Sheriff Doyle and his posse.

Happy drew in his reins and stopped his lathered-up buckskin mount, then eased himself carefully off the saddle and down on to the ground.

He rested against the saddle of his tired horse and watched his fellow Bar 10 riders copying his actions. It had been nearly three hours since they had set out from the heart of the Bar 10.

The horses walked into the cool water and drank as their masters rested on the banks of the fast-flowing river.

Happy managed to get the feeling back in his legs at last, and walked to the exhausted cowboys. Gene Adams had sent Rip Calloway, Larry Drake, Billy Vine, Don Cooper and Josh Weaver to help the sheriff of Silver Springs. None of them, with the exception of Rip Calloway, was an expert with his guns, but all were capable of handling a stampeding herd.

Adams knew that Sheriff Doyle would bring enough deputies with him who were more than capable of using their weaponry against the rustlers if they showed themselves. His men would ensure that if the white-faced cattle of the combined herds stampeded when the shooting started, they would be controlled and not allowed their head.

'Sure glad that the days are longer this time of year.' Happy sighed as his eyes studied the sky above them. 'I'd hate to be riding this trail in the dark.'

'What's this all about, Happy?' Rip asked.

'We're going up on the northern range to help Sheriff Doyle and his men stop them darn rustlers, Rip,' Happy replied as he rubbed his aching spine with gloved hands.

'But that ain't Bar 10 land, is it?' Josh Weaver queried.

'Nope.' Happy pulled out his tobacco pouch and loosened its drawstring.

'Then how come we have to go there and help Doyle?' Billy Vine chipped in.

''Coz Gene told us, that's why.' Larry Drake spat at the ground and unscrewed the stopper of his canteen. 'Steers have been rustled up there by varmints from the Badlands. They might get ambitious and try and steal ours next.'

'But it ain't our steers that have been rustled. I don't get it,' Don Cooper said, rubbing his drooping white moustache. 'Them ranchers up on the range ain't even friendly. What does Gene wanna help them for?'

'Hush up,' Rip said. He checked his Peacemaker carefully and slid it back into its holster. 'We don't get paid to ask dumb questions. We do what Gene tells us. He pays the bills and that makes him head honcho.'

'Exactly,' Happy agreed as his tongue slid along the gummed edge of the cigarette paper.

'How many rustlers are there?' Billy

Vine asked, a troubled tone in his youthful voice. 'I don't cotton to being faced by a couple of dozen gun-toting outlaws. I'm a wrangler and that's about all I'm good at.'

'Gene knows our strengths and weaknesses, Billy boy.' Happy grinned as he tucked the cigarette in the corner of his mouth. He struck a match on the grip of his gun and cupped the flame to the tip of the smoke. 'He must want us to make sure that we control them white-faces.'

'Then how come we got so much hardware and bullets?' Josh asked. 'If we were just going there to look after the steers, then why are we laden down with enough guns, rifles and bullets to take on the cavalry?'

'Just in case we have to defend ourselves, I guess.' Rip shrugged.

'But we ain't gunmen,' Billy said nervously. 'Why didn't he send Johnny? Johnny can shoot the eye out of a squirrel at a hundred paces.'

'I can use this old hogleg.' Rip patted

his holster. 'I reckon I can shoot as straight as Johnny.'

'Me too!' Happy said. A stream of smoke drifted from his mouth.

All five seated cowboys laughed.

'Sure ya can, Happy!' Don Cooper joked.

'Just make sure that if Happy draws his gun, you're standin' way behind him.' Rip smiled.

Happy Summers rested a hand on his ample belly, then checked his pocket-watch.

'Darn. I'm hungry.'

'Ya always hungry,' Rip commented.

'We ain't got time to rustle up no grub,' Larry Drake said. He finished the water in his canteen, then rose to his feet and headed to the river to refill it. 'It's a hard ride to Cripple Creek from here and we ain't got much daylight left.'

Happy inhaled deeply, then tossed the last half inch of his cigarette into the water behind him.

'Larry's right. Fill up ya canteens and

we'll head on to meet up with Doyle.'

Billy Vine followed the older Bar 10 men to the river's edge and filled his canteen. He was shaking from head to toe and Rip Calloway noticed it. The tall cowboy moved closer to the youngest of Gene Adams's ranch hands.

'I'm scared, Rip,' Billy whispered.

Rip patted the youth on his back.

'We're all scared, Billy boy,' Rip said. He gathered up his long reins and grabbed the horn of his saddle.

'Yeah?'

Happy Summers walked to his horse and looked hard at the youngster. His smile lit up the distance between them.

'Rip ain't joshin', Billy. Only a fool wouldn't be a tad scared when faced with the unknown.'

Don Cooper hoisted himself atop his cutting horse and steadied the tired beast with expert hands.

'You stick close to Happy, Billy boy.'

Billy mounted and turned his horse.

'You reckon Happy will protect me, Don?'

Don laughed.

'Nope. But he's so darn fat, we could all hide behind him if the shootin' starts.'

The riders headed north along the river again.

5

There was an atmosphere within the Bar 10 ranch house which tainted every bite of the meal Gene Adams had before him. His mind could not stop thinking about the six loyal cowboys whom he had sent to help Sheriff Ben Doyle. For Adams was a man who hated letting others do something that he felt he ought to have done himself. Sending Happy and the others north, even with enough weaponry to start a small revolution, still troubled him. The meal had gone virtually untouched. Adams pushed the plate away from him and then used the napkin to wipe his mouth. He could not face the well-cooked steak supper. He had no appetite.

Cookie wandered in from the kitchen and stared at the large steak on the rancher's plate, but did not utter a word. He had known Adams and Tomahawk for twenty years. The expert chef knew that the rancher was a complex character who considered every one of his cowboys as the children he had never been fortunate enough to have been blessed with.

Tomahawk gave a knowing nod to the cook, who returned the unsaid message. The cook went silently back to the kitchen.

'What's eatin' you, Gene?' Tomahawk asked at last from across the large table. 'You ain't even touched the meal Cookie made.'

Johnny Puma had eaten most of his supper and was leaning back in his chair trying to allow his food to go down.

'It was darn good, Gene. Honest.'

The rancher looked up at his two best friends and tried to smile. None came to the tanned features.

Johnny reached to his cup and drank the last of the black coffee, then reached for the tall black pot and poured himself another. He too had noticed the way Adams had been brooding all through their nightly meal.

'You want that last biscuit, Tomahawk?' Johnny asked.

'How can you eat when ya can see that old Gene here is fretting, boy?' Tomahawk asked. He watched the rancher rise to his full height and make his way across the large room towards the massive fireplace. Adams bent over, picked a log from the high stack and tossed it into the roaring fire.

'I've always found it strange that even in the hottest of summers it gets cold this time of night, boys.' Adams rested an elbow on the high mantel and stared down into the flames.

Tomahawk moved away from the table and made his way to his favourite chair. He rested his thin frame on the soft cushions and looked hard at the face he had known for more than four decades.

'You're worried about Happy and the boys, ain't ya?'

Adams gave a slight chuckle.

'Never have been able to fool you, have I?'

'Nope. Not in all the darn years we spent together. I can read ya like a book.' Tomahawk watched Johnny walking to his own chair and winked at the youth.

'How long have you known each other, Gene?' Johnny asked, staring through the steam of the coffee cup at his lips.

'It's hard to say, Johnny.' Gene Adams straightened and then allowed the fire to warm his rear. 'How many years is it, old-timer?'

Tomahawk scratched his beard and tried to work out the answer. He did not have enough fingers.

'That kinda depends on what year it was that we met.'

'Well?' Johnny leaned forward in his chair. 'What year did you meet, Gene?'

Tomahawk's expression became serious.

'I'm darned if'n I can recall that. But

it don't make no difference though.'

'Why not?'

''Coz I ain't too sure what year it is now,' Tomahawk admitted.

Adams lowered his head, walked across the room and stared out of the largest of the many windows in his ranch house. He rested his gloved hand on the back of one of the numerous hardback chairs which furnished the huge room.

Johnny was about to speak to the rancher when he noticed Tomahawk's thin index finger pressed to his whiskered mouth, warning him to remain silent. The young man had come to consider Adams as the father he had never had. He began to drink his coffee.

'Is there a moon, Gene?' Tomahawk piped up.

'Nope. Just a million Texan stars,' came the reply.

Tomahawk turned in his comfortable chair and studied the rancher. He knew more about the big man than any other living soul. There were no secrets between them after so many years riding the same trail. Their lives had become joined together and they both knew that only death could alter that.

'You sure that them's Texan stars, Gene?' Tomahawk's eyes twinkled in the lamplight. 'I done heard that some of them are Mexican!'

'Reckon you could be right, ya old fool.' Adams sighed. 'But the biggest ones are Texan.'

Tomahawk nodded.

'Sure enough. Stands to reason.'

Gene Adams inhaled deeply until his chest almost popped the buttons on his black shirt.

'I'm starting to worry if I did the right thing sending Happy and those boys to help Doyle.'

It was an admission that Tomahawk had been expecting.

Johnny looked over the back of his chair.

'Maybe I should have gone with them, Gene. If there is any gunplay, I'm far better with my Colts than any of the boys. I could have handled a bunch of low-life rustlers.'

'You're hot-headed, Johnny,' Tomahawk said bluntly. 'Happy don't get so riled up as easy as you do.'

Adams nodded. He looked out at the buildings and stock pens bathed in the light of a score of lanterns.

'Johnny's right, Tomahawk. I reckon I ought to have sent him with them. They need a good gunhand if the trouble starts. Maybe I should have gone too.'

Tomahawk slid his famed Indian axe from his belt and waved it around his head.

'You should have sent me, Gene. I can kill anything with this here backscratcher. I've saved your bacon enough times.'

Gene Adams turned and faced the two men. His expression was grim as he sat down on the hardback chair next to the window.

'Maybe I've made a darn big mistake, boys. One that might cost lives. The lives of our boys.'

Tomahawk jumped to his feet and ambled to the rancher's side. He rested a hand on his broad shoulder.

'Listen up, Gene. You sent our best wranglers to help Sheriff Doyle. Men who can keep even the most skittish herd of steers in check. Even white-faces. That's what you done. Rip knows how to use his gun if he has to, but Doyle's men are the ones who are gonna do any real shootin' if'n there's a call to start shootin'.'

Gene Adams looked up at Toma-hawk's ancient face. Even though hardly a tooth was left in the mouth that hid behind the whiskers, he could see the comforting smile in the wrinkled eyes.

'Remember when we first came into this land?' Adams asked in a low whisper.

Tomahawk nodded. 'Yep. All them darn Indians and Mexicans trying to keep this place for themselves. It was like we never stopped fighting long enough to get us a cooked meal.'

'Remember the gal I was sweet on, old-timer?' Adam's voice lowered so that only Tomahawk could hear his words.

'The sweet little thing in the wagon train? Gosh, she was somethin' special, weren't she? What was her name?'

'Amy.' Adams's voice broke. 'Amy Jones.'

'She was darn pretty, Gene.'

'She was before them Apache's attacked the wagon train.' There was agony in every word that came from the rancher's lips. 'That was my fault!'

Tomahawk squeezed the broad shoulder.

'No it weren't, boy.'

Gene Adams turned and stared out of the window into the blackness.

'If only I hadn't made that one mistake, Tomahawk. That Apache war party would not have . . . '

'We was scouting for the wagon master, boy. Looking for a safe route through the mountains. We couldn't have stopped those Apaches even if'n we'd been with them. There was too many of them. Remember all them pony tracks we found when we got back to the wagon train? There must have been a hundred or more.'

'All I remember is burying her and her folks, Tomahawk.' Gene Adams shook his head.

Tomahawk leaned closer to Adams. 'If we'd been with the wagon train, we'd have not stood a chance either, Gene.'

'Maybe. Maybe not. Who knows?' Adams sighed and looked up into the ancient cowboy's face. 'All I know for sure is that I didn't just bury her that day. I buried my heart too.'

'That must be nearly forty years back, Gene.' Tomahawk sighed. 'You've built this ranch and helped a lot of youngsters turn into fine men along the way. You never once hurt no one unless they hurt you first.'

Adams thought about the corner of his immense cattle ranch that was covered in blue-bonnet flowers. A sacred place where he buried his dead beneath the natural splendour of countless flowers. The exact place where the wagon train had met its fate nearly forty years earlier. The place where he had buried his beloved Amy.

'I've made some mistakes over the years and they've proved costly,' Adams said in a regretful tone. 'I should have gone with the boys to help Doyle.'

'They don't need wet nursing!' Tomahawk insisted. 'They're Bar 10 men.'

'I sure hope that you're right.'

'So do I, Gene. So do I.'

Johnny Puma got to his feet and looked at the two men. He had never seen either of them like this before.

'What you two talking about over there?'

Gene Adams stood and patted Tomahawk's back.

'Mistakes, Johnny. We was talking about mistakes.'

6

The range was almost flat beyond the million-acre Bar 10. Knee-high grass swayed beneath countless twinkling stars as the dozen horsemen moved their mounts ever onward towards the Red River border to the lawless Oklahoma territory.

The distinctive white faces of the grazing beef cattle could be seen above the high grass in every direction. They seemed to gather in large groups, as if there was safety in numbers. It was a strange sight for Gene Adams's cowboys to see cattle without horns which could span more than six feet from one deadly tip to another.

The cowboys were used to seeing the flashing of the distinctive long horns as they caught the sun, moon or starlight across their polished surfaces back on the Bar 10. It was said that white-faced steers gained more weight in less time than the native Texan longhorn, but Adams cared little for them. He had spent his entire adult life creating the finest herd of prime longhorns in the state and cared little for making a little extra profit.

His riders of the Bar 10 felt the same. A steer had to have horns and that was that. The creatures that grazed the open range were strange beasts. They seemed out of place.

As they rode in a straight line across the huge range, the cowboys kept their eyes on the white-faced cattle that moved amid the ocean of grass. Did they stampede like real cattle? Each of the six Bar 10 horsemen wondered if these beasts could ever be as dangerous as their own stock.

Sheriff Doyle and his five-man posse did not give the steers a second thought. They watched with keen eyes for any hint that the rustlers had returned yet again. It was two-legged animals which they worried about.

The eerie starlight troubled the experienced lawman. There was no moon and seeing anything clearly was almost impossible.

The darkness offered no comfort to any of the twelve riders.

Every one of them knew that the men they sought could already be here on the vast range with the sights of their Winchesters trained upon them. Even dim starlight could find the metal bridles and exposed guns and rifles.

Whoever the rustlers were, they had to be ruthless to be living in the territories, the sheriff thought. Only those skilled with their guns lived long enough to become that bad. Doyle wondered if he and the men in his charge might be a tempting target.

There was a low moaning noise from the great beasts which drifted on the evening air. It chilled the twelve riders as they got closer and closer to the Red River. It sounded like a million phantoms rising from their graves.

Was this an omen of things to come?

Were the dead trying to warn the living of dangers as yet unseen? None of the dozen riders could relax for even a second. The blood-chilling sound ensured that they listened.

'I don't cotton to this place,' Don Cooper said to Billy Vine as they rode side by side at the back of the posse.

'Me neither, Don.' Billy gulped.

'Hush up back there!' Happy ordered over his shoulder.

Then another sound traced over the long grass and filled their ears.

This was a different sort of noise: the noise of fast-flowing water as it cut through its well-carved route.

Happy Summers spurred his cutting horse closer to the silent Doyle's side. The two men led the ten other horsemen closer the the sound of the big river.

Doyle raised a hand and pointed ahead.

Happy nodded when he too saw the starlight dancing on the water in the distance. It was less than a mile ahead of them, flanked by well-nourished trees, trees that seemed to stretch as far as the horizon as their deep roots sucked the precious liquid from the winding length of the Red River.

Nature itself had made this border and it was an awesome sight to the saddle-weary group of horsemen.

'There it is, Happy,' Doyle said across the distance between their two cantering mounts. 'Beyond them trees is the so-called Badlands.'

'But them cattle-rustlers could come in from the Badlands anywhere along the river, Sheriff,' Happy muttered. They drew closer to the noise of the lapping water as it coursed along its chosen route. 'How are we meant to guard the length of such a river?'

'A thousand men couldn't guard that,' Larry Drake piped up as his cutting horse eased alongside the lawman.

Doyle pulled back on his reins and halted his mount. He glanced all around him until satisfied that every one of the men in his charge had also stopped.

'You're both right. We can't cover it all. Nobody could,' Doyle said quietly. He pulled out a long cigar from his jacket pocket and raised it to his mouth.

'Then this is impossible.' Happy shrugged. He rested his wrists on the saddle horn before him and took the weight off his ample rear.

'Gene wouldn't have sent us here if he thought that, Happy,' Larry told his fellow-cowboy.

Doyle bit the tip off the cigar and spat it at the ground, then placed the long Havana between his teeth.

'There ain't too many places where anyone could drive a lot of cattle across the Red River up into the territories, boys.'

'There ain't?'

Doyle pulled out some matches and carefully extracted one from the wooden box.

'There's maybe three spots that're

shallow enough for cattle to ford this river. The closest to the Badlands is straight in front of us.'

Happy looked to where the lawman's long finger was pointing. To him, it looked exactly the same as the rest of the tree-lined river.

'What's over there in the Badlands, Sheriff?'

'You'd be surprised, son. There's a few towns left over from when it was Indian land. The Indians never stopped whites from going in there and setting up settlements. Why should they? They done OK from the deal.' Ben Doyle scratched the match across the edge of the box, cupped the flame in his hands and sucked in the strong smoke until his lungs were filled.

'I don't understand,' Happy admitted.

'Me neither,' Doyle said. Smoke drifted through his teeth and disappeared into the darkness that surrounded them. 'Things were pretty peaceful until the folks back East stuck their noses in. Reckon them politicians want to bring in a whole heap of farmers. Farmers are easier to control than Indians.'

Suddenly a noise came from the right of the twelve mounted riders, a noise that echoed across the silent range. At first it seemed like the rumbling of a distant thunderstorm. But there were no clouds in the sky above them.

Rip Calloway hurriedly moved his horse next to the sheriff and pointed.

'Look!'

Every eye squinted in the direction that Rip was aiming his gloved finger at.

'What is it?' Doyle asked, steadying his horse and trying to make out what Rip was so concerned about. 'What you pointin' at, son?'

Before Rip could reply, the sound of gunshots rang out across the vast range. Then the rumbling grew even louder.

Happy stood in his stirrups and screwed up his eyes until he was able to focus.

'Holy smoke!' he exclaimed. 'It's them rustlers. They're driving a whole bunch of steers straight at us.'

Doyle turned and looked at Happy. Even in the light of only the stars, he could make out the sheer horror that etched the normally smiling face.

'Are you sure, Happy?'

Happy gathered up his reins until there was not one inch of slack. He held his skittish gelding in check as only a skilled wrangler could and spat at the ground.

'I sure am, Sheriff!'

'What'll we do?' Doyle returned his attention to where Rip had indicated. His eyes could still not see anything.

'We have to find cover and fast,' Happy shouted above the ever-increasing noise. 'There's a lotta steers heading to the river, boys. Maybe hundreds. And we're right in their path!'

Ben Doyle held firmly on to his reins. The ground was indeed shaking. He could feel it beneath his saddle. Then more shots filled the air.

'We'll be killed for sure,' Doyle yelled.

'Not if we can find some place to

protect us and our horses, Sheriff!'
There was now urgency in Rip's voice.

'We gotta get out of here!' Don Cooper shouted over the shoulders of the terrified deputies between himself and the sheriff. 'They'll wipe us out if'n we don't.'

Happy turned the head of his buckskin cutting horse and aimed its nose at the river.

'C'mon!' he yelled to his fellow-riders. 'Let's try and find us some cover, boys!'

None of them needed telling twice. The dozen men spurred their mounts and drove their horses hard towards the dark trees that marked the river's edge.

Following Happy blindly through the tall grass, the desperate riders urged their mounts on as they heard the sound of hundreds of white-faced cattle closing in on them.

With every heartbeat, the herd gained on the cowboys and posse. Rip Calloway leaned over the neck of his charging horse but never once took his eyes off the steers that were making the ground shudder, the closer they got to the dozen startled horsemen. The sky lit up as the rustlers fired their guns up at the stars.

Happy spurred his buckskin and hauled back on his reins. He felt the muscular animal leap across the wall of brush in front of him and then land on the softer ground that led down towards the raging river.

There were trees all around him as he steadied the loyal gelding. He looked over his shoulder and watched as his fellow Bar 10 men managed to get their horses to jump the bushes. Then he saw the posse driving their mounts straight through the dark brush. He pulled hard on his reins and then urged his mount to go left as the remaining riders caught up with him.

'This way!' Happy called out frantically.

The riders trailed him into the heart of a dense thicket of trees. They were surrounded by enough wood to build a small fortress.

More shots rang out in the night air.

The horrific sound of frantic white-faced steers grew louder and louder as the twelve horsemen dismounted quickly and tied their reins to the sturdy trees.

'Will these trees be strong enough to stop them steers from knocking them down, Happy?' Doyle shouted into the ear of the rotund cowboy.

'Reckon we'll find out pretty darn soon, Sheriff.' Happy pointed at the ground above them. Countless snorting cattle broke through the undergrowth and came hurtling down the steep slope toward them. 'Look!'

Doyle and the others all stared at the terrifying sight and saw the riders who were driving the cattle off the range and towards the river.

'The rustlers!' Ben Doyle cried out to the men all around him. 'Get ya guns out, boys. We gotta stop them varmints before they get across the river.'

The posse and cowboys quickly hauled their carbines from their saddle scabbards and pistols from their holsters when the sheer size of the rustlers' rampaging herd became evident. At least 200 white-faced steers tore through the brush above the posse and crashed down as they tried to flee the men firing their guns behind them.

'There they are!' Doyle pointed the barrel of his carbine at the horsemen as they came into sight at the top of the slope.

The rustlers were waving saddle ropes and screaming at the tops of their voices in between squeezing their triggers, to keep the huge animals moving.

Dust off the backs of the cattle filled the air. Doyle gripped his Winchester in both hands and leaned against one of the trees. Within seconds, he could see nothing as the heavy steers crashed feverishly into the wall of tall pines.

The twelve men had nothing to aim at.

Happy Summers moved to the sheriff's side and screwed up his eyes in a vain attempt to see through the choking dust.

'This ain't good,' he yelled above the sound of the noisy herd. 'I can't see the rustlers, Sheriff. I can't see nothing at all.'

'We can't see the critters but I can sure hear them,' Doyle said, listening as the men continued to shoot. 'Hark.'

'Yeah,' Happy agreed as he too heard the rustlers through the wall of dust.

'Shoot high, boys,' Ben Doyle ordered loudly as more and more steers crashed into the trees and scrambled around the thicket. 'Over the heads of the cattle. We might get lucky and manage to pick off some of them thieves.'

It was not an easy order to obey. The men began to fire their weapons high but knew that the steep slope that they had travelled down to reach this relatively safe haven made it impossible for them to be sure where their bullets would end up.

The sound of the cowboys' and posses' blazing guns soon brought the return fire of One-Eyed Jake McGraw and his outlaws. Suddenly, it was the Fourth of July.

White-hot tapers of venomous lead cut through the dust and rained down into the tall trees and all those who were taking cover there. A million splinters showered over Doyle and his trapped men.

Josh Weaver screamed and staggered into Happy Summers. He tried to cling to the large man but his fingers had lost their strength. He slid to the ground.

'Josh?' Happy gasped as he dropped to his knees and checked his friend.

'Is he . . . ?' Doyle began to ask.

'Yep. He's dead,' Happy answered. He lifted his rifle to his shoulder and started to fire repeatedly up into the choking dust. 'Ya gonna pay for this!'

Even more of the outlaws' deadly bullets rained down.

The horses whinnied as some of the bullets tore into them. Horses pulled desperately at the reins that held them firmly in check as the lethal lead tore in among them.

Then it was clear that the last of the rustled steers had gone past them and reached the fast-flowing Red River.

The air began to clear of dust but soon filled with gunsmoke instead as bullets went continuously in both directions. Men screamed out on both sides as deadly bullets found their targets in the darkness of night.

Doyle moved from one tree to another, trying to avoid the ceaseless shower of lead that was coming in from at least a half dozen directions.

'We're sitting ducks, Sheriff!' Rip Calloway shouted as he tried to reload his Colt for the third time.

'Rip's right. They'll pick us all off if we don't get out of here, Sheriff,' one of the posse raged, firing his rifle at their unseen enemy.

'Just keep shooting, boys!' Doyle ordered. 'Shoot in the direction that their bullets are coming from.'

Two of his posse had already fallen at

his feet. They lay lifeless in the churned-up ground as the cowboys moved to try and protect their horses from the ceaseless volleys of outlaw lead.

'Where are they?' Billy Vine cried out as he clung to his six-shooter near one of their wounded mounts. 'How can I shoot at them if I can't see . . . '

The words of the youngest Bar 10 cowboy faded into a chilling silence. Don Cooper raced across the distance between them and jumped over the body of a stricken horse.

'Billy boy?' Don called out as he pushed himself into the dead wood under the trees and used his hands to search for the youth.

'What's wrong, Don?' Rip called out as even more bullets tore the bark off the trees above his head.

'It's Billy, Rip,' Don Cooper shouted.

'What ya mean?'

'He's dead!' Don replied. 'Billy's dead. Them varmints have killed little Billy.'

Rip Calloway could see the shape of Don Cooper rising from the side of their fallen friend with his gun in his gloved hand.

'Stay down, Don!' Rip yelled out.

Don Cooper squeezed between two tall pines and then began to make his way up the slope. With every step he was firing into the gunsmoke-thickened air.

'Show yourselves, ya cowards.'

One-Eyed Jake McGraw moved from his hiding-place and squeezed the triggers of both his Colts. He did not wait to see the cowboy fall but grabbed the reins of his mount and hauled himself back into his saddle.

'C'mon, men. We got us a herd to catch up with.'

Sheriff Doyle and his men ducked as the outlaws fired, riding down the slope and across the river.

Rip Calloway broke cover and rushed to the body of Don Cooper lying face down in the mud. He cradled the lifeless cowboy in his arms and stared hard into the faces of the men who had survived.

'Is he dead, Rip?' Happy asked as he reached the kneeling cowboy.

'Yep,' Rip answered. 'He's dead just like Billy and Josh and them deputies, Happy.'

Happy Summers pushed his Stetson off his sweating brow and gazed into Ben Doyle's face as he staggered towards them.

'You OK, Sheriff?' Happy asked, noticing the grim expression carved into the lawman's features.

Doyle did not reply. He just looked down at his chest and touched the neat hole that had gone through his vest a mere inch away from his star. His knees buckled and he too fell face first into the mud.

8

It had been the longest night that Gene Adams had ever lived through. He had decided that he could not just ignore his instincts. The tall rancher knew in his heart that he had to ride north and find his men and Sheriff Doyle. He threw his saddle-bags over his broad right shoulder, opened the solid wooden door, crossed the porch and descended into the morning light. He glanced across at the noisy rooster that was heralding another new day atop the henhouse and made his way straight towards the large barn.

Adams had not managed to get even a fleeting moment of sleep during the hours of darkness. Somehow he knew that something was wrong.

Every sinew in his body told him that he had probably sent six of his best cowboys to their deaths. He knew that he had no reasons to explain his anxiety but for sixty years his instincts had never once let him down.

Gene Adams knew that he had to go to them.

There simply was no other way.

To ignore his feelings would be to betray everything that had made Adams the man he was.

The entire ranch was still asleep but that did not bother him. He preferred it that way. He had made up his mind and there was no one alive who could stop him. If he could ride out before any of his men awoke, he would not have to explain himself to them.

Not have to justify his actions.

Adams walked into the barn and along the line of stalls until he came to the one where his prized chestnut mare stood. The animal watched her master approach and nodded her head up and down as if she could read his mind.

He unclipped the rope that spanned the front of the stall and led the eighteen-hands high horse out into the centre of the large building.

'You knew I was coming here, didn't you, girl?' Adams asked the mare as he dropped the saddle-bags and plucked the bridle off the wall. He carefully manoeuvred it over the chestnut's handsome head. Her eyes were still as clear and alert as they had been the first day he had saddled her up more than a decade earlier. 'I reckon you know what I'm thinking before I do myself.'

As if in answer, the horse snorted.

'Maybe after all these years I ought to have given you a darn name,' Adams mumbled as he tossed the blanket over the back of the mare and patted it down. 'Something rather better than just calling you girl all the time.'

The chestnut's ears pricked forward as Adams tossed the heavy saddle on top of the blanket and then made sure that it was sitting correctly.

'Would you like a real name, girl?'

The horse turned her head. She was looking at the open doorway of the barn. Adams reached under her belly, caught hold of one of the Texan cinch straps and brought it up to its fastening.

'What you seen?' Adams asked, finding the second strap and securing that too. 'We got company?'

The distinctive figure of Tomahawk appeared in the doorway with the sun on his back.

'What in tarnation are you doin', Gene?'

Gene Adams straightened up, placed his saddle-bags behind the cantle, then led his quiet mount out into the light of the new day.

'I'm going up to the northern range, old-timer,' Adams said as he led the mare to the nearest trough and allowed the animal to drink.

Tomahawk, only half-dressed, followed the rancher.

'What for?'

Adams removed two empty canteens off a fence where more than a score of them were hanging. He handed one to Tomahawk, then unscrewed the stopper of the other.

'Help me fill these canteens, old-timer. I don't want to waste time stopping for water on my ride to the boys. It'll take me long enough to reach the range as it is.'

'You serious about going up to the range?' Tomahawk asked, fumbling with the canteen's stopper.

'You bet I'm serious,' Adams replied. He leaned one hand on the handle of the water pump next to the trough. 'I shouldn't have sent them boys up there without tagging along myself. After all, it was my idea.'

Tomahawk watched as Adams pushed the pump handle up and down several times before the fresh water began to flow freely from the spout.

'If'n you're dead set on heading up there, wait for me to get dressed and my horse saddled up,' the old man said. 'I could wake Johnny and we could all go. There's enough hands here to take care of business. They won't miss us for a few days.'

'You boys have work to do around

here, Tomahawk,' Adams said putting the stopper back on his full canteen.

'What work? There ain't nothin' that can't wait for a couple of days.' Tomahawk accepted the full canteen in exchange for the empty one. He watched Adams pumping the fresh water into that one as well. 'Cookie can run this place as good as we can.'

Adams raised a dark eyebrow. 'Cookie can run anything better than you.'

Tomahawk ambled closer to the tall rancher.

'C'mon, Gene. Me and young Johnny could tag along, huh?'

'How long would it take for you and Johnny to get ready?' Adams asked his old friend.

'Five minutes?'

Adams stopped pumping and thoughtfully screwed the stopper back on the second canteen. He knew that Johnny and Tomahawk had grit. Enough grit to have saved his life as many times as he had saved theirs.

'OK. Go wake the young 'un up,'

Adams agreed. 'I reckon I could use the company. If I'm wrong about Happy and the boys needing my help, I ain't gonna look so stupid when I turn up if you're with me.'

'Nobody looks stupid if they stand next to me.' Tomahawk winked. He ran across the distance between the barn and the ranch house like a man half his age. The rancher smiled as he hung the canteens on his saddle horn.

'Looks like we're gonna have us some company again, girl,' he muttered. 'Still, there's one thing for certain with them two riding with us. They can't get into any trouble if they're with me.'

Gene Adams was checking that his Winchester was fully loaded when he caught sight of the two men rushing out of the ranch house and heading towards him.

'Ain't we gonna have us any breakfast, Gene?' Johnny asked, buckling up his gunbelt and tying both leather laces around his thighs.

'I'm a tad hungry myself, Gene,'

Tomahawk added, pulling his battered hat over his unkempt hair until the tops of his ears bent over.

'I packed us a few sandwiches, jerky and hard-tack,' Adams said. He looked at the handsome youngster as he rushed into the barn after Tomahawk.

'Did *you* make the sandwiches, Gene?' Tomahawk shouted out from inside the dark building.

'You bet I did,' Adams called back. 'Why?'

Tomahawk led out his black gelding and began securing its saddle.

'I've tasted your sandwiches before, boy,' Tomahawk mumbled under his breath.

Johnny walked out into the morning sun with his pinto pony following close behind him.

'What's wrong, Tomahawk?' Johnny asked.

'Gene made sandwiches, Johnny.' Tomahawk's words sounded like a warning to the youth.

'Yeah?' Johnny rubbed his chin and

then stared at the tall rancher. 'Is that right, Gene? Did you make 'em?'

Adam's expression changed.

'OK. Go and get Cookie to make you some sandwiches of your own.'

Tomahawk's eyes twinkled as he headed back to the ranch house.

'It ain't that we don't like the way you make sandwiches, boy. But when it comes to food, you're a darn good cattle rancher.'

Gene Adams sighed heavily.

'Just hurry up,' he shouted.

Johnny cleared his throat. 'Can I go and get me some of Cookie's sandwiches too, Gene?'

'OK. I guess Cookie's grub is a mite more edible than mine, Johnny,' Gene reluctantly conceded. 'But hurry up. It's a long ride to the northern range.'

Johnny finished buckling his cinch straps and then followed Tomahawk towards the house. He was staring up into the cloudless sky when something caught his eye to his right. The young cowboy stopped in his tracks, rested his wrists on his gun grips and stared out beyond the white fences that ringed the middle of the Bar 10 ranch.

'Hey, Gene.'

'What, Johnny?' Adams looked across at the young man and moved away from the chestnut mare. 'What are you looking at, son?'

'Somebody is heading in.' Johnny raised his right arm and pointed. 'Look at all that dust being kicked up over yonder. We got company.'

'Uninvited company.' Gene Adams strode to the cowboy's side and looked off in the direction he could see Johnny's eyes were focused on.

'Who do you reckon it is?'

'Could be trouble,' Gene said through gritted teeth. 'Maybe you ought to wake up the rest of the hands. We might need to make a fight of it.'

'There ain't enough time, Gene.'

Adams knew that the young cowboy was right. There was not enough time to do anything but stand and wait.

'Reckon so, son.'

Johnny rested his hands on his gun grips.

'I figure it must be at least five or six riders, Gene.'

'You're right. That's a darn sight more dust than any one rider would make, Johnny. An awful lot more dust and that's for sure. Who are they?'

'Whoever they are, they managed to get past our outpost,' Johnny observed.

Gene Adams reluctantly flicked the safety loops off the hammers of his golden Colts and continued to stare at the dust. The riders were heading towards the heart of the Bar 10. They were coming in really fast, he thought.

'Can you make them out, boy?'

'Not through the heat haze, Gene,' Johnny replied anxiously as he stood square on to the shimmering images.

Gene Adams patted the young cowboy's shoulder.

'Whoever they are, they're definitely headed here.'

'I'm ready, Gene.' Johnny flexed his

fingers above the grips of his holstered guns.

Adams continued to stare at the approaching dust.

'We're both ready, son.'

9

The tortured expressions that were carved into the features of Johnny Puma and Gene Adams were almost identical as they suddenly realized who the riders who were approaching them were. Adams stepped forward in disbelief and momentarily clenched both gloved hands.

'It's the boys!' the rancher said.

Johnny inhaled deeply, then cleared his throat. He tried to speak but no words came from his lips. It felt as if there was a noose strangling him.

The five dishevelled horsemen were all that was left of the men Happy Summers and Sheriff Doyle had led into the northern range.

'Oh dear Lord!' Adams exclaimed in horror as the sudden realization of what he was witnessing overwhelmed him. 'Look at the bodies, Johnny.'

'Look, Gene.' Johnny swallowed hard. 'Half of them are dead.'

'I'm looking, Johnny,' the rancher somehow managed to say as he focused beyond the few familiar faces and on to injured horses with seven bodies draped across their saddles.

Both men rushed across the white sand towards the exhausted riders. It was obvious that these horsemen had been riding since the previous night. They were like the remnants of a battle that none of them had expected to fight.

Happy Summers tried to dismount, but fell heavily on to the dry ground. He lay at his horse's feet and just kept shaking his head.

Adams knelt at the big cowboy's side and hauled the heavier man off his face. He rubbed at the trail dust which covered Happy's stunned features.

'Take it easy. You're home, Happy. You're back on the Bar 10, son. What happened?'

'They stampeded a couple of hundred white-faced steers into us, Gene.'

Happy sighed as he felt the strong arms of the rancher encircle his shaking shoulders. 'We didn't stand a chance. We were taken by surprise.'

'How many are dead, son?' Adams managed to ask as his eyes flashed around the other mounted men.

'Sheriff Doyle and three of his deputies are dead,' Happy gasped as Johnny handed him a full canteen.

Gene Adams helped Happy drink a few precious mouthfuls of the cold liquid.

'And our boys?'

Happy pulled the canteen from his lips and looked right into the face of the man he respected above all others. The pain was carved into his features.

'They killed little Billy and old Don. Josh is dead too. Only me, Rip and Larry managed to survive the outlaws' bullets along with two of Doyle's deputies, Gene.'

Gene Adams helped Happy to his feet and steadied the confused man in his arms. His eyes glanced at the two surviving deputies, who were both wounded.

'You men get yourselves to the ranch house,' Adams told them. 'Cookie will tend your wounds and feed you until we can get a doctor out here.'

The deputies both staggered toward the ranch house. Neither of them seemed capable of speaking. Their eyes were glazed as if they were unable to come to grips with what they had endured.

'Get your pony, Johnny!' Adams growled. 'Ride to Silver Springs and bring back Doc Parker. Tell him we've got two deputies and three cowboys who need patching up.'

Johnny touched the brim of his Stetson.

'Right away, Gene.'

Adams held the young cowboy's arm and looked straight into his handsome face. 'And tell the undertaker to bring seven of his best coffins here.'

Johnny Puma nodded silently. Adams watched the youngster race across the ground to the waiting pinto and leap on to his saddle. The youngster turned the head of the handsome animal and spurred hard. The pony galloped eastward towards the distant town.

Tomahawk came out of the ranch house with two small bundles of sandwiches in his bony hands. He said nothing as the two deputies made their way past him into the building.

'Get over here, old-timer,' Adams shouted at the stunned Tomahawk, who stared in disbelief at the unexpected sight which greeted his ancient eyes.

Tomahawk hurried to the grim-faced rancher's side.

'What in tarnation happened, Gene?'

'We got our tails kicked, Tomahawk,' Rip Calloway muttered as his feet touched the ground for the first time in more than five hours.

'The rustlers did this?' Tomahawk gasped.

'They sure did.' Happy nodded. 'I never seen such shooting in all my days. They picked us off at will. They could have finished us all off if they hadn't decided to catch up with them white-faced steers.'

'Them steers went into the Badlands just like all the others, Gene,' Rip added.

Tomahawk was about to speak again when he saw the seven bodies hanging over the saddles.

'H . . . how many of our boys were killed, Happy?'

'Three, Tomahawk,' Happy answered reluctantly.

'You recognize any of them rustlers, boys?' Adams asked.

Larry Drake sat on the ground and rubbed the trail dust off his face.

'Nope. But there was one of them who had an eye-patch.'

'There can't be too many outlaws with only one eye,' Adams said under his breath. 'I'll find him. I swear it. I'll make him and his gang pay for this.'

Gene Adams let go of Happy and then turned to look at the bodies which hung limply over the saddles. It was a heart-breaking sight. Slowly he walked to the injured mount that had Billy Vine across its saddle.

Without uttering a word, the rancher untied the ropes that secured the young cowboy's body to the horse and then gently hauled the lifeless Billy off the saddle.

He cradled the dead boy in his strong arms and walked towards the ranch house. He paused for a second beside Tomahawk and cleared his throat.

'Bring the rest of boys into the house, Tomahawk.'

'Yes, Gene,' said Tomahawk quietly.

Every eye watched as Gene Adams strode towards the ranch house with Billy Vine in his arms.

No one said a word.

10

Frank Davis, Sol Knight, Jeb Barnes, Bobby Lee Jones, Jess Hart and Zane Quinn trailed the awesome figure of One-Eyed Jake McGraw into the outskirts of Cheyenne Creek. The stench of death lingered upon them like the flies which found the mindlessly discarded garbage that always littered such towns. The seven riders had done their work well and left the two hundred white-faced cattle on their ranch west of the busy town.

Now they were ready to celebrate.

For they had nearly doubled the size of their stolen herd overnight. The deadly gang had lost one of their group during the heated and unexpected encounter with Sheriff Doyle and his eleven supporters. Yet like the vermin they were, they had already forgotten their fallen colleague as if he had never even existed.

For that was what vermin did.

Their entire existence was governed by instinct and bore no relation to anything remotely human.

One-Eyed Jake's head moved constantly as he guided his horse towards the large wooden building with the words GOLDEN GOOSE SALOON painted on a large board above the overhanging roof of the porch.

The town was alive with outlaws and those who lived off the backs of them. Of all the towns that had been left in the Indian Territory, Cheyenne Creek had become the most popular because of its close proximity to the Texas border.

There were few towns as dangerous as Cheyenne Creek. With more than a thousand of the country's most dangerous outlaws living within its boundaries, and no law of any kind, only those who lived by their expertise with their guns survived here.

McGraw liked this town and had decided that of all the notorious outlaws who walked its board-walks, he alone would become its undisputed leader.

Soon he would control Cheyenne Creek.

His singular form of madness ensured that his ambition would never waver until he had achieved his goal. The outlaws who filled the Badlands simply used this place as a safe haven from the law that sought their lives. One-Eyed Jake McGraw knew that there was far more to be had from the newly named Oklahoma territory. From here it was possible to strike out at all the neighbouring states and territories and bring their ill-gotten gains back to a place from where no one could legally retrieve them.

Gangs of the most dangerous men and women who had ever drawn breath had already staked their claim to every square inch of the notorious Badlands, but McGraw had clawed out the largest chunk for himself.

This was one place where the meek did not inherit the earth.

Only the ruthless and strong ruled here.

And there was no one more ruthless than the man with the eye-patch. For he had an advantage over all the other outlaws who had taken refuge here. Insanity had made him feel that he was totally invulnerable.

One-Eyed Jake McGraw had taken the lion's share of the land on the outskirts of Cheyenne Creek and used it to fatten up his newly acquired steers until the cattle agents from Kansas drifted south to purchase them.

The agents would not ask any questions if the carefully adjusted brands fitted those found in the official cattle-breeders' guide.

And One-Eyed Jake knew that his Triple X brand would fit.

McGraw had done his homework and registered his own brand with the correct authorities, using the dubious services of a tame lawyer.

He knew every brand south of the Badlands and had designed his own so that more than half of the Texan ones could easily be altered to resemble his own Triple X brand.

One-Eyed Jake now had enough prime Texan cattle to make him the wealthiest of all Cheyenne Creek's inhabitants. Dividing his time between his ranch and rooms in the town's best hotel, he knew that it was only a matter of time before the Kansas cattle agents responded to his numerous tempting telegraph messages and letters.

The East required as much beef on the hoof as the West could provide. And McGraw knew that the agents would not be able to resist the chance of laying their hands on his newly acquired herd of white-faced steers for ever.

Not if he sold them for half the price that the Texan ranchers would have to charge.

The infamous outlaw drew in his reins and dismounted from his lathered-up horse outside the saloon.

He had lost one man during the brief but bloody encounter with Sheriff

Doyle but neither he nor his six remaining men could care less.

McGraw walked up the steps to the boardwalk outside the Golden Goose saloon. He struck a match along the nearest wooden upright and stared around the busy street and at his grim-faced followers.

'We ought to be crowned king or somethin', Jake.' Quinn laughed heartlessly. 'We must have more than five hundred head of cattle now.'

McGraw did not reply. He sucked in the strong smoke and stared hard with his one good eye at the group of men who were approaching them from the opposite side of the wide unnamed street.

Bobby Lee Jones noticed the expression on the cruel face of his leader and turned to look at what McGraw's attention was fixed on.

'It's the Reno Kid and his gang, Jake!'

'I seen them,' McGraw growled under his breath. He tossed the spent match aside and sucked even harder on the long black-leafed Havana.

'You bin getting a little too big for ya boots, Jake,' the Reno Kid shouted as he and his men came to a stop in the centre of the busy street.

'Ya reckon?' McGraw moved to the front of his six men and rested both hands on the grips of his guns.

The Reno Kid was a man with greying side-whiskers who seemed to have outlived any reason to have the word 'kid' in his name. He had killed more than a score of men in his time and was noted for his speed with his single Remington. He was a man who had been the most feared resident in the Badlands until McGraw arrived.

'We reckon that now you and the scum you ride with ought to hand those cattle over to us.' Reno grinned across the distance between them.

'You figure?' McGraw inhaled the thick smoke of his cigar.

'Yep. I figure,' Reno said.

Jeb Barnes moved toward the edge of the boardwalk.

'There are a lot of crazy gun-happy saddle tramps in town.'

'Darn right, Jeb.' McGraw grinned and pointed the tip of his cigar at the men standing before them. 'And there are most of them.'

The Reno Kid glanced to right and left at his gang. They fanned out more widely and all placed their hands on the grips of their weaponry.

'I figured that you thought I'd ignore the fact that you've bin trying to take over in Cheyenne Creek, Jake,' Reno began. 'But I just bin waiting for you and them clowns of yours to round up all them steers off the range. Now you have, I'm taking over. OK?'

McGraw pulled the long cigar from his teeth and exhaled.

'Not likely, Reno.'

Reno seemed to be surprised by the fact that none of the men who faced him and his own gang appeared to be scared. He had built a reputation that was known throughout the West and yet these men were smiling at him.

'I thought you had more brains than this, Jake,' Reno said in a cold tone that chilled the air. 'You wanna die?'

'I ain't gonna die, but you and ya boys are.' One-Eyed Jake arched his neck and spat a lump of black goo across the street. It landed on the highly polished left boot of the Reno Kid.

McGraw's men began to laugh.

'You darn swine!' Reno screamed at the top of his voice. 'Let them have it!'

Within the blinking of an eye, every one of the men who faced each other had drawn their guns and started to fire. The air was filled with acrid black smoke as deadly bullets tore through the hot morning air. One-Eyed Jake dropped down off the boardwalk with one of his Colts in his hand. He ducked under the gunsmoke and then blasted all six bullets into the legs of Reno and his gang.

The Reno Kid fell to the ground and watched as the rest of his followers began to spin on their heels and land all about him.

McGraw's six outlaws followed their leader and threw themselves into the dust at his side. Their guns blazed. There was no mercy from any of them.

As Reno fell back he saw the awesome sight of One-Eyed Jake rising and coming towards him. The Kid tried to rise but his legs were filled with bullet holes that oozed red gore over his once immaculate boots.

Resting on one elbow, the Reno Kid raised his Remington and pulled back on its hammer. He squeezed its trigger and watched as his last bullet ripped the Stetson off the approaching man's head.

Blood traced down from the graze on the top of McGraw's scalp but the crazed outlaw kept advancing.

'You won, Jake. OK?' Reno shouted as he realized that he was watching his own executioner get closer and closer with every beat of his pounding heart.

One-Eyed Jake did not reply. He

continued to move towards the helpless Kid. Then, as he reached the stricken outlaw's side, Jake holstered his Colt.

'You're the winner, Jake. I'm done for.'

McGraw smiled and licked the blood that trickled into his mouth. It tasted good, he thought.

'You ain't quite finished, Reno.'

The expression on Reno's face altered. He had never faced a madman before. He looked all around him at the bodies of his own gang and then at the empty Remington in his hand. He tried to lash out with the weapon but McGraw just tore it from his grasp.

'Scared, Reno?'

'What ya gonna do, Jake?'

McGraw slid the long knife from his boot and grinned.

'I'm gonna cut ya heart out and ram it down ya throat, boy.'

Before the Reno Kid could say another word, the long blade had been thrust into him. His eyes widened as he felt the lethal knife being expertly twisted inside him.

Death came slowly to the outlaw.

The smell of stale smoke and heavy sweat filled their nostrils as the six outlaws trailed One-Eyed Jake McGraw into the saloon.

More than fifty other outlaws filled the large saloon. They parted like the Biblical Red Sea as the seven men made their way straight to the long bar.

The three bartenders abandoned their other customers and all gathered, waiting to serve the famed one-eyed killer.

'Whiskey,' McGraw ordered, placing a handful of silver coins on the wet surface of the bar counter. 'Seven bottles of ya best whiskey, barkeep.'

The coins were covered in blood.

It was the Reno Kid's blood.

The bartenders all jumped into action and gathered seven bottles of the best whiskey the Golden Goose had to offer.

There was no one who could or would challenge them.

'I like the Badlands.' One-Eyed Jake laughed. 'It's quiet here.'

11

It was a sight that the owner of the Bar 10 had seen many times over the previous forty years. But that had been before the legal confusion had created the infamous Badlands out of the Indian Territory. The Red River had always formed the border carved out by nature or God which separated two very different kinds of terrain. Gene Adams eased back on his reins and stared at the wide river before him. He stroked the neck of the tall chestnut mare with his gloved right hand and then adjusted his white hat.

Adams had forsaken his usual ranching clothes to try and disguise himself from knowing eyes. He knew that there was only one way to get the better of ruthless outlaws, and that was to try to appear as bad as they were.

There had been two choices. He

could either try to appear even lower than the deadly outlaws were themselves, or attempt to make them believe that he was superior to all of them in every way.

Gene Adams had chosen the latter course of action. He was trying to look like the most sophisticated man that any of the outlaws in the Badlands had ever seen. A cross between a river-boat gambler and a ruthless cattle buyer's agent.

He was dressed in a fawn-coloured frock coat and dark trousers. A frilly white shirt and black string tie sat behind a silk double-buttoned vest.

Gene Adams checked the shoulder holster which he had exchanged for his usual gunbelt. The single golden-plated Colt sat hidden under his left arm.

He had encountered a lot of card-sharps and unscrupulous cattle agents over four decades and knew if anyone could convince deadly rustlers that he was what he professed to be, it was Gene Adams.

As long as no one recognized him, he might survive.

His mature looks helped. No one lived as long as he had without being good with a gun or lucky.

Or both.

Glancing down into the fast-flowing water, he could make out his own shimmering reflection. For a brief moment, even Adams thought he was looking at someone else.

It was now or never. He had made up his mind.

He inhaled deeply and then gently tapped his spurs to encourage the mare to continue.

'C'mon, girl. Let's go find us some cattle-thieves.'

Gene Adams had a plan. One that he knew might end up costing him his own life. But one which was his best chance of getting the better of the cattle-rustler who wore an eye-patch, and his deadly followers.

The chestnut mare walked into the Red River elegantly. Its master allowed the horse to find its own route. Half-way across the horse began to swim until its hoofs found the ground again.

Once upon the other side, Gene Adams knew that he was alone.

Totally alone.

There was no law here.

But a lawless range did not frighten him. Adams was old enough to recall a time when Texas was exactly like that. Men survived by their own strength and ability to fight. He had lost none of his willpower.

The rancher thought about the sheriff's star he had hidden in the lining of his frock-coat. A star which he knew was meaningless in the lawless territory which faced him, but one he could and would use when the time was right.

He had forced the mayor of Silver Springs to give him the sheriff's star the previous day, when he had escorted the bodies of Ben Doyle and his deputies back to the quiet town.

Gene Adams had been racked with guilt.

A guilt he knew would haunt him for the rest of his days if he did not do something to try and make amends. He knew that he had innocently sent Ben Doyle and the others to their premature deaths.

He owed them!

Gene Adams was a man who always paid his debts.

The chestnut moved quickly through the lush countryside. It was an easy trail to follow and he decided that he would see where the rustlers had taken the herd of white-faced steers before trying to find the outlaws.

The deeper he travelled into the strangely quiet land, the more he recognized it.

Adams had been here many times before when the land was more peaceful. He had even driven several trail drives through this territory with the permission and blessing of the Indians who had once lived here. It had cost a few dozen steers, but that was a small price to pay for a safe journey to

Kansas with several thousand head of longhorns.

The further north he rode, the more familiar the landscape became. Adams knew almost every hill and valley from here to the Kansas State line.

Suddenly, as he rode around a tree-covered bend, he found himself faced by two grim-faced horsemen holding Winchesters across their laps. They seemed to be guarding the churned-up trail from curious eyes.

Adams hauled in his reins and slowed the mare until it stopped directly before the two men.

'Howdy, boys.' Adams smiled and touched the brim of his new hat.

'Git going, dude,' one of the men gruffed.

'But why?' Adams smiled. 'I'm a cattle agent from Kansas.'

The two men looked at one another and then back at Adams.

'Cattle agent?' the second rider asked. 'Did One-Eyed Jake McGraw send for you, dude?'

The name traced up and down Adams's spine. He could hardly believe his luck at having been given a name to fit Rip Calloway's description of their adversary.

'That's the gentleman. He sent my company a wire,' Adams lied.

'How come ya heading up from the south if'n Jake sent you a wire in Kansas, mister?' the first rider asked. 'Kansas is north of here, ain't it?'

Gene Adams had to think quickly.

'Exactly right, my friend. I was in El Paso when my company wired me from Kansas and instructed me to come and have a word with Mr McGraw about his herd.'

The two men shrugged.

'OK. You stay on this trail and you'll end up in Cheyenne Creek. The herd is grazing just west of town,' the first man said.

'Thanks, boys.' Adams touched his hat again and continued his ride. He increased his pace as the aroma of cattle grew stronger and stronger on the otherwise crisp air.

Adams recalled the town called Cheyenne Creek which one of the horsemen had mentioned. He knew that the infamous outlaws who now dominated this territory must have taken over it and all the other deserted towns. That had to be where he would find the man he sought.

One-Eyed Jake McGraw!

The powerful chestnut mare continued galloping for another few miles, then reached the top of a high tree-covered ridge. The Bar 10 rancher pulled back on his reins and came to a halt. He stood in his stirrups and stared down at the grazing herd. At least four or five hundred of them were contentedly grazing on the vast fertile range below his high vantage point.

It was a far bigger herd than he had imagined. The rustlers had been very busy, he thought.

Gene Adams took a mouthful of water from his canteen and then returned it to his saddle horn. The trail wound down the steep hill and then went off to his right just as the men who'd questioned him had said.

He had found the steers. Now all he had to do was find the men who had stolen them.

Adams pulled the reins to his right, turned the head of his magnificent horse and spurred hard. He galloped down the steep hill and rode on in the direction of Cheyenne Creek.

He was about to play the most dangerous game of poker of his entire life.

The stakes would be high.

They might even cost him his life.

12

Cheyenne Creek looked the same as it had the last time Gene Adams had ridden through its unnamed streets. But he could sense that it was no longer a place where decent folks lived. On every corner he recognized the faces of men who, until now, he had only seen on Wanted posters.

Men who seemed amused by the sight of someone wearing their Sunday best. Adams smiled at every face that looked in his direction. He knew that even deadly killers could be taken off guard by a smile.

The line of horses outside the Golden Goose stretched half-way around the large building. Adams decided that if he were to find the one-eyed man, it was more than likely he would be in a saloon celebrating his latest crime. Aiming his horse at the biggest saloon in Cheyenne

Creek seemed the most obvious way of tracking McGraw down.

Yet as the rancher steered the chestnut mare down the middle of the main street towards the aromatic drinking den, he noticed that curious men were starting to follow him. He began to wonder if they knew something that he did not.

This might prove to be his greatest challenge, he thought. He had to pretend that he was unafraid even though faced by countless guns on the hips of the gathering crowd.

Adams reined in and dismounted. He looped his reins around a small space at the end of a hitching-pole and then walked behind a dozen horses towards the saloon steps.

With every step, the crowd grew bigger and closer.

Gene Adams tried to ignore them. He climbed the steps to the boardwalk and walked through the swing-doors into the saloon, but he knew that they were still trailing him.

The Golden Goose was only half-full as Adams made his way towards the long bar and the waiting trio of bartenders. He noted that four men were sat near a window, playing poker; there was an empty chair.

'What'll it be, stranger?' The oldest-looking of the bartenders asked, leaning both elbows on the highly polished surface.

'A tall beer will do just fine,' Adams replied, watching the crowd following him into the saloon. 'I seem to have gathered a few moths to my flame.'

'Just watch ya back,' the bartender whispered.

'Are they dangerous?' Adams asked in an innocent tone.

'Everyone in this town is darn dangerous, stranger,' the man muttered. He placed the beer down in front of the rancher and leaned even closer. 'Most of them are just back-stabbing scum, but some are real gunfighters trying to make a reputation for themselves.'

'Is that so?' Adams sipped at the beer

and glanced at the poker-playing men again. He then looked at the crowd, which seemed to be content just to watch him, the same way that vultures watch an animal, waiting for it to die.

'Only yesterday morning the Reno Kid and his gang tried to make a name for themselves by drawing on One-Eyed Jake.' The bartender's expression told the story long before the words dripped from beneath the handlebar moustache. 'They all got themselves killed.'

Adams frowned.

'This One-Eyed Jake character is good with his guns, I take it?'

'And his knife.' The man shuddered.

'Knife?'

The bartender lowered his head.

'He cut out Reno's heart, stranger. Cut it out and rammed it into the Kid's mouth.'

Gene Adams swallowed hard. He had heard of many things in his sixty years of life, but nothing like that.

'Are you serious?'

'Yep. Jake McGraw's a maniac,' the

man whispered. 'When he ain't killing or stealing all he does is play poker over there near the window. If he loses, he gets real upset. He killed the last man to beat him.'

Adams took another mouthful of beer and then pointed at the card-table where the players were finishing a game.

'Is he there now?'

'Nope. He ain't come in today yet. That's his chair next to the wall. Nobody sits there unless they want to get themselves beaten up or worse.'

Gene Adams smiled even more broadly as he reached into his vest pocket. He pulled out a handful of golden eagles and began to toy with them.

'I think I'll ask those gentlemen if I can sit in for a few hands, barkeep. I like a game of poker.'

The bartender moved along the long bar.

'Are you ready to die, stranger? You can't sit in McGraw's chair and live.'

Adams touched the brim of his hat.
'Just watch me.'

The four card-players watched as Gene Adams pulled the chair back and sat down. He smiled at the four stunned men.

'Mind if I sit in, gents?'

One of the group rubbed his face and loosened his collar as his eyes darted around the large saloon.

'Are you loco, stranger? That's Jake McGraw's chair. Nobody sits in his chair.'

'Well, he ain't here, is he.' Adams's expression changed. He was suddenly serious. 'I want to play poker. The question is, do you?'

Another of the men began to twitch nervously. 'But he will be here at any moment, dude. He always comes in about this time to play cards. He'll kill ya for sure if he sees you sitting there. Get going while ya still can.'

Adams placed the gold coins down.
'May I have some chips please?'

The man who was closest reluctantly

took the coins and pushed a tall pile of chips in front of the Bar 10 rancher.

'We warned you.'

'That you did, friend. And I'm much obliged. The thing is that I've never met a two-eyed man who frightened me. No one-eyed critter could even make me break into a sweat.'

The cards were shuffled and dealt across the green baize.

The game had started.

Every man in the Golden Goose wondered if it might just be the stranger's last.

13

The note that Gene Adams had left in his Bar 10 ranch house had been found by Tomahawk just after dawn. Tomahawk's worst nightmare had become a reality. Adams had gone alone to the Badlands against the wishes of all his loyal friends.

The old-timer quickly awoke Johnny Puma. Both men read the emotionless note together and had been chilled by the words it contained.

Dear Tomahawk and Johnny,

I've given this an awful lot of thought over the last couple of days. But whichever way I added it all up, I came to the same conclusion.

It's up to me to try and get the killers of our boys and Sheriff Doyle and his deputies. I went to see the mayor of Silver Springs yesterday and he agreed to my request and made me the new sheriff. I have a warrant to arrest the rustlers which I will use if I get the chance. These killers will pay for what they have done.

So I've headed to the Badlands. Do not follow me, boys. This is my problem and I shall try my best to solve it alone. If anything happens to me, look after the Bar 10, boys.

Your friend
Gene.

Tomahawk and Johnny had been told not to follow. That was the one order that neither of them could obey. They doubted that the rancher thought that they would obey. He knew them as well as they knew him.

The two Bar 10 riders drove their mounts hard across the northern range towards the Red River. Neither knew when Gene Adams had actually left the ranch but both hoped that it had only been a short while before they had found his letter.

If Adams had left only an hour or so earlier than themselves, there was a good chance that they would catch up with him before he got into any real trouble.

It was a vain hope, but one that both horsemen silently clung to as they got closer to the river border.

Johnny hauled back on his reins and stopped his pinto pony at the very edge of the river. The ground was churned up where the rustlers had driven the hundreds of white-faced cattle across the river.

The wily Tomahawk drew alongside his young pal, slid off his saddle and knelt at the water's edge. His keen eyes studied the cut-up ground where the steers had been driven only two nights earlier.

To the untrained eye, it looked like just a muddy mess.

Johnny Puma leapt from his pony and moved to the side of the crouching old man.

'Nobody could make sense of that,

Tomahawk,' Johnny said as he watched the man rise back to his feet. 'The ground is too beaten up.'

'Gene crossed here, Johnny,' Tomahawk said, pointing at the muddy ground. 'I figure he's less than a few hours ahead of us.'

The young cowboy watched Tomahawk remount his black gelding. He moved to the head of the snorting horse.

'Are you serious, old-timer?'

'You bet I am,' Tomahawk replied. He gathered up his reins and rubbed his whiskered chin. 'He went through there just after dawn, I tell ya.'

Johnny nodded. He walked to his pinto, grabbed the mane, threw himself on to the saddle and straightened up. He knew that Gene had told him a hundred times that the old man had been raised by Indians and lived with them until he was an adult. Tomahawk had learned all the skills that most Indian braves took a lifetime to master and could track anyone over any terrain. His accuracy with the lethal Indian hatchet had made him legendary.

'You lead the way, Tomahawk,' Johnny said. 'If anyone can find Gene, it's you.'

'Ya darn tootin', boy.' Tomahawk's eyes wrinkled up.

Just at that moment Johnny noticed something and held his pony in check.

'Look back there. Somebody's coming after us fast.'

Tomahawk stood in his stirrups and stared at the land behind them. He pointed a bony finger.

'Can your young eyes see who that is trailing us, boy?'

Johnny Puma turned his pinto and raised a hand to shield his eyes from the bright sunlight.

'I sure can make out a few of them, Tomahawk.'

'Then who is it?'

'I can make out Happy and Rip and a lot of other riders coming in fast.' Johnny sighed. 'Must be every one of the Bar 10 boys by the looks of it.'

Tomahawk shook his head.

'Gene'll be mighty angry about that.'

'What ya mean?'

'Well he told us not to follow him and we done ignored him. Right?' Tomahawk sighed.

'Right.'

'Now we got the rest of the ranch following us. Gene'll go loco, I tell ya.'

'Reckon you're right but what can we do?' Johnny glanced up at the riders who were getting closer.

'I dunno.'

Johnny held tightly on to his reins as the thirty or more riders stopped their horses right next to them.

'Where ya going?' Rip Calloway asked.

'We was trailing Gene,' Tomahawk answered. 'Where was you headed?'

'We was following you two,' Happy Summers said.

Tomahawk shook his head.

'But Gene don't want us to trail him into the Badlands, boys.'

'Then why are you trailing him?'
Larry Drake grinned.

Tomahawk scratched his beard again.

''Coz me and Johnny know that he
don't really mean for us not to trail
him. He needs us really but is too darn
stubborn to admit it. There are too
many of you boys.'

'How can there be too many of us,
old-timer?' Rip queried.

'Me and Johnny are gonna sneak in
there. Them outlaws would spot a
bunch like you a mile off.' The bearded
man waved his arms around like a
windmill. 'A bunch like you might
make it dangerous for old Gene. We got
savvy. We've mixed with that sort before
and know how they think. Two men
have a chance of reaching Gene but not
all you critters.'

Happy eased his buckskin horse next
to Johnny Puma's and looked into the
youngster's eyes.

'What do you reckon, Johnny?'

'Tomahawk's right.'

'Then what'll we do?' Happy asked.

His fingers pulled out his tobacco pouch from his shirt pocket. 'Seems kinda dumb to just head on back after we come all this way.'

'Stay here and wait.' Tomahawk winked.

'Wait for what?'

'For one of us to give you further instructions,' Johnny said. 'You boys make camp here and either me or Tomahawk will give you orders when we know what's happening. Gene must have some sort of plan under his hat and when we know what it is, we can act.'

'OK. We'll wait here,' Rip drawled.

'Good. Now you boys make camp someplace where there's cover in case them rustlers come back here.' Tomahawk laughed as he steered his horse into the river with Johnny following his on his pinto pony.

'If we don't hear nothin' from you boys in two days, we're coming in after you,' Happy shouted after them.

'You do that, boy,' Tomahawk called back over his shoulder.

14

The seven outlaws made their way along the busy street from the hotel towards the Golden Goose. They had slept until nearly two in the afternoon and then decided to get themselves a drink. A really big drink.

As always, One-Eyed Jake McGraw led his gang with an aggression that defied any sane man's logic. He pushed people aside as if they were mere flies waiting to be swatted.

The busy main street was filled with buckboards and riders going about their daily routines, but all stopped their horses to allow the gruesome one-eyed outlaw uninhibited access from one side of the street to the other.

As they reached the boardwalk, bathed in blinding sunlight, Frank Davis tapped McGraw's shoulder.

McGraw swung around and pushed

the barrel of one of his guns into the throat of the big outlaw.

'Never touch me, Davis!'

The terrified Davis nodded then raised his arm to point down the street at an approaching horseman.

'I just wanted to tell ya that one of the men we left on the trail to guard our stock is riding in, Jake.'

McGraw lowered his pistol and spun it on his index finger until it slipped into his right holster. He smiled, patted the face of the taller man and turned his head so that his one eye could see the rider.

'What's he doin' here? I paid them both to stay out there until I told 'em different.' McGraw stepped down off the boardwalk as the horse was reined in.

Without any warning, One-Eyed Jake grabbed at the man in the saddle and hauled him to the ground. The stunned man tried to speak but the back of both of McGraw's clenched fists hit his head one way and then the other. Blood trickled from the stunned man's mouth as he fell to his knees.

'When I gives an order, folks obey!' McGraw snarled like a mad animal. 'Right?'

The kneeling man raised both his hands to shield his face.

'Right, Jake,' he mumbled.

One-Eyed Jake roared with laughter. There was no humour in the laugh, only more evidence of his total insanity.

'Now tell me why ya come to town when you knew that I give ya orders to stay with the herd on the trail?'

The man continued to keep his hands raised in case more blows rained down on his swollen face.

'Have ya seen him?'

'Seen who?' McGraw leaned forward.

'The dude who says he's a cattle-buyer from Kansas,' the man explained. 'I just wondered if he might have gotten lost on his way to town. He passed me and Luke about three hours back. We thought he might get himself lost 'coz he looked like he'd never been outside on his own before, Jake.'

McGraw grabbed the kneeling man's collar and hoisted him back to his feet.

'A cattle-buyer?'

'Yep. He looked like a gambler. Rode a real tall chestnut mare.'

Sol Knight moved closer to the drooling McGraw.

'There's a darn pretty chestnut mare tied up outside the Golden Goose, Jake.'

Jake McGraw released his grip on the bleeding man and walked towards the chestnut horse as if he were in a hypnotic trance.

'At last! One of them Kansas cattle-buyers has come to buy our steers from us.'

The injured man staggered to a trough and buried his head in the cold water whilst McGraw's six henchmen trailed their leader closer to the magnificent animal tied among so many inferior horses outside the saloon.

'A darn good horse,' Jake McGraw said.

'Worth taking and keeping.' Jeb Barnes grinned as the rest of the gang studied the animal.

The haunted expression on the face of the one-eyed outlaw bore like a drill into Barnes. McGraw was not amused and slapped the face of the outlaw as he passed and made his way up the sun-bleached saloon steps.

'We don't steal from someone who might make us all rich, at least not until he's paid us.'

The six outlaws followed McGraw to the swing-doors where he had stopped and was looking into the crowded bar room.

'That must be the critter, Jake,' Bobby Lee Jones said.

'Yeah! He's the only dude in here,' Jess Hart added.

Jake McGraw's face began to redden. His breathing increased in pace until his chest was like a blacksmith's bellows.

'Something wrong, Jake?' Quinn asked.

'He's sitting in my chair!' McGraw shouted.

Every man inside the Golden Goose stared in terror at the sight of the one-eyed outlaw striding into the large room with his gang trailing him like ducklings following their mother.

The four men at the poker-table dropped their cards and were about to flee when Adams raised his own voice menacingly.

'Stay where you are, gentlemen. No harm will befall you this day.'

McGraw was like a raging bull as he snorted his way up to the card-table and stood above the elegantly dressed Gene Adams.

'That's my chair!'

'These folks already told me that, Mr McGraw,' Adams said staring up from beneath the brim of his new white hat at the almost purple face. 'I've been sitting here for a couple of hours now and have grown used to it.'

'Did they also tell ya what I do to folks who sit in my chair, *amigo?*'

One-Eyed Jake raged.

'They did.' Gene Adams looked up at the face and narrowed his eyes.

'And you still sat there?'

Gene Adams had not blinked once since he started talking to the angry outlaw.

'Certainly. I see no reason to miss a good game of poker simply because of a silly reason like this being your chair. Find yourself another chair.'

McGraw's hands moved towards his gun grips.

'I wouldn't do that if I were you, Mr McGraw,' Adams advised, swiftly drawing his golden Colt from the holster that hung hidden under his left arm. His thumb cocked the hammer and he smiled.

One-Eyed Jake's jaw dropped. He had never seen anyone draw a gun so quickly.

'Who are you, dude?' He asked.

'The name's Smith. You've probably heard of me.' Adams smile widened as he watched the one-eyed man's gang

135

retreat to the long bar counter.

'You got a big family,' McGraw said, lowering his hands down to his side.

'There are quite a lot of us.' Adams released the gun hammer and then holstered the weapon swiftly. 'You want to play cards?'

McGraw grabbed the neck of the nearest poker-player and threw him to the floor.

'I'll sit here. Give me five hundred dollars' worth of chips.'

One of the other players took the paper money from the outlaw and slid a pile of chips to him. McGraw stacked them in front of him.

Gene Adams gathered up the cards from the table and shuffled them.

'Are you the cattle-buyer?' McGraw asked.

'Indeed I am.' Adams smiled as his hands dealt the cards to the four other men seated around the round table. 'It's quite flattering to think that you know of me so soon after my arrival in your nice little town.'

'How come you wear a glove on ya right hand, Smith?'

'This is my eye-patch, Mr McGraw. If you get my drift.' Adams replied. He rested the remainder of the deck on the table.

The outlaw leader nodded.

'I get ya drift.'

Each of the players placed a dollar in the middle of the table, then picked up their five cards and held them to their chests to study their hands.

McGraw smiled and tossed a hundred dollars worth of chips in the middle of the green baize.

'This'll separate the men from the boys.'

'Too rich for me,' one of the other players said, throwing his cards down.

'And me,' another agreed.

'Smith already won most of my money,' the third said. 'I fold.'

'Looks like it's just you and me.' Gene Adams fanned his cards and studied them carefully. He lifted five twenty-dollar chips and placed them next to the the others on the table.

McGraw licked his lips.

'Getting interesting.'

'Indeed.' Adams nodded and placed another five chips in the pot. 'And I raise you another hundred.'

'You must have a good hand, Smith,' McGraw said. He picked up another ten chips and dropped them on the growing pot. 'Your hundred and another hundred.'

Adams nodded.

'You need any cards?'

'Two.' McGraw said. He removed the bottom pair of cards and tossed them away from him.

Adams lifted the deck and gave his opponent two cards.

'I'll take one card.'

One-Eyed Jake watched as the man opposite gave himself a card after throwing one away.

Both men studied their new hands. McGraw now had three queens, a ten and a nine. He smiled, then noticed the blank expression on Adams's face.

It was all the encouragement the deadly outlaw required.

'Wanna quit, Smith?'

'I'll raise you another two hundred,' Adams said, to the outlaw's surprise.

McGraw watched as the chips were pushed forward. He looked at his own dwindling pile of chips, inhaled deeply, then added them all to the pot.

'OK?'

Adams smiled once more. 'I'll raise you another thousand.'

There was a hushed silence as Adams's words rang around the saloon. None of the men who were watching the game could believe their ears.

'A thousand bucks?' McGraw gasped angrily.

'Indeed, Mr McGraw,' Adams confirmed.

Both men stared at the cards in each other's hands. McGraw patted his pockets and could not find more than a couple of fifty-dollar bills. He wanted to kill the smiling Adams but then remembered that this was a man who claimed to be a cattle-buyer and he needed to sell his rustled herd.

Reluctantly he placed his own cards down.

'It's your pot, Smith. Take it.'

Adams placed his hand on the table and pulled all the chips toward him.

'Thanks, McGraw.'

'But I would like to see what beat me,' One-Eyed Jake said grabbing Adams's cards and turning them over.

Adams watched silently as he saw the expression on the outlaw's face change. McGraw went crimson when his eye focused on Adams's cards.

'Two fives?' Jake McGraw raged furiously. 'You beat me with a pair of fives?'

'That I did,' Gene Adams replied.

'Ya stole that game from me!' McGraw pushed himself away from the table and stood. His hands grabbed at his holstered gun grips.

Adams rose to his feet and drew his own Colt. He pushed it into the outlaw's face.

'Keep them holstered or I'll surely kill you.'

15

The afternoon sun was hotter than Hell itself. Its rays bleached every building in Cheyenne Creek mercilessly as the two Bar 10 riders at last came to the end of their quest. It seemed to Tomahawk and Johnny that every man, woman and three-legged hound dog was headed toward the large saloon. The boardwalks were already creaking under the sheer weight of the people who were trying to see into its shadowy interior.

'What ya reckon is going on there, boy?' Tomahawk asked as he trailed the pinto around the horde of excited people.

'I don't know,' Johnny admitted. 'But I reckon that it has something to do with Gene.'

'Ya could be right,' Tomahawk agreed as his younger friend pulled back on his reins and turned the pony.

'Follow me, old-timer,' Johnny said over his shoulder; a split second later he spurred the horse into action.

'There he goes again!' Tomahawk grumbled to himself. 'Like a firecracker on the Fourth of July.'

The pinto pony mounted the boardwalk and squeezed its way down the narrow gap between two buildings. The black gelding followed close behind.

'Where we going, Johnny?' the older man asked loudly.

Johnny reached the alley and guided his mount quickly past the back of two buildings until he came to the rear of the Golden Goose saloon. Johnny turned his mount around and watched his confused pal reining in beside him.

'We're going inside the saloon!'

Tomahawk scratched his beard.

'But why?'

'Didn't ya see Gene's horse out front, Tomahawk?' Johnny dismounted and tried the rear door of the building. It was locked up tight.

'Locked?' Tomahawk asked. He slid off his saddle and came to Johnny.

'Bolted on the inside!' Johnny fumed before taking a few steps backward and studying the tall building.

'What ya looking at, son?'

'Look up there.' Johnny pointed to an open window directly above the rear door. It was at least sixteen feet above them. 'That's our way in.'

'I can't get up there, boy,' Tomahawk protested.

Johnny shrugged.

'Well, I've gotta get into this saloon anyway. I reckon Gene's in there and he might be in trouble.'

'But how are ya gonna get all the way up to that window, Johnny?' the older man asked.

There was no reply. Johnny grabbed the bridle of his pinto and led the animal to the door. He grabbed his saddle rope and uncoiled it until he was able to make a loop. Then the athletic youngster climbed up on top of his saddle, balanced carefully, and started to swing the rope full circle.

Johnny allowed the loop to get bigger gradually as it rotated around in his skilled hand. He had roped countless longhorns in his time on the Bar 10 but had never tried anything like this.

When the rope was twirling at full speed, Johnny released the loop and watched it glide heavenward. It caught around a wooden joist protruding from the roof.

'Got it!'

The Bar 10 cowboy triumphantly pulled the rope until the loop tightened around the joist.

'Will it take ya weight?' Tomahawk queried.

'Heck, I ain't as heavy as Happy,' Johnny said, wrapping the slack of the rope around his arm.

'Be careful.'

'Follow me up, Tomahawk,' Johnny said. He climbed the taut rope until he reached the open window. Hanging by one arm, he pulled the sash window upward until it opened fully. The cowboy allowed himself to swing back and forth and then raised his right leg until the spurs dug into the soft wood of the sill.

Using this hold to anchor himself for a moment, Johnny stretched out and hauled himself into the dark room.

Tomahawk muttered under his breath as he tried to get on top of the pinto pony.

'Stay still, ya darn stupid horse.'

Johnny's head jutted out of the window. 'Are you coming or not, Tomahawk?'

Tomahawk screwed up his eyes and stared at his friend.

'You find a way down from there and then unbolt this darn door!'

Johnny smiled. His head disappeared into the room. The sound of cowboy boots racing down a wooden staircase echoed from inside the building. The bolts were released and the door opened up.

'That was gonna be my second suggestion, old-timer. C'mon.'

16

'Leave ya guns holstered, boys,' One-Eyed Jake ordered his six men as they edged away from the long bar towards the man who had a golden gun pressed into their leader's face. 'He ain't gonna kill me. Smith's bluffin' again, just like he did with that pair of fives.'

Gene Adams raised one of his dark eyebrows.

'I ain't bluffing this time. I will blow your head off if you try to draw those guns, McGraw.'

For the first time the outlaw realized that Adams was deadly serious. Even with only one eye, he could see that there was no emotion in his opponent's face.

'I reckon you're serious, Smith.'

'Deadly serious,' Adams said in a hushed tone.

The six outlaws continued to move towards them.

'Stay back!' McGraw shouted angrily at his gang. None of them seemed to listen.

'We can take him, Jake,' Bobby Lee Jones said.

'Trust us, boss,' Quinn added.

For the very first time in his life, Jake McGraw felt that he might die through no fault of his own.

'Stop, ya dumb bastards!' McGraw yelled as he felt the cold barrel of the golden Colt being pushed deeper into his face. 'I don't wanna end up in Boot Hill just because you fools think you can take him.'

Suddenly two voices came from behind the six outlaws. Tomahawk and Johnny were moving from the back room of the saloon towards them.

'Pluck them guns out of them holsters and drop them on the floor, boys,' Tomahawk ordered, waving his .45 at the backs of McGraw's men. 'I got me a hair trigger and my finger kinda twitches when I'm excited.'

'You ought to listen, boys,' Johnny grinned, holding his pair of matched Colts in his steady hands. 'Drop those guns.'

Slowly the surprised outlaws lifted their guns out of their holsters, using only fingers and thumbs. They dropped them on to the sawdust-covered floor.

Gene Adams stepped backwards and glanced across at his pals.

'I wondered when you two would show up.'

One-Eyed Jake McGraw felt his hearbeat slowing down inside his large chest.

'Who are they, Smith?'

'Two of my associates, Mr McGraw,' Adams answered. 'They are experts in the cattle department.'

'But I thought you were the cattle expert?' McGraw said.

'I deal in the financial side of the business.' Adams pulled out the guns from the one-eyed outlaw's belt and threw them across the room.

McGraw stared at the golden pistol.

'What's that mean, Smith?'

'It means that I handle the money.' Adams smiled and slid his pistol back into its hiding-place.

Tomahawk moved to the side of the tall rancher.

'No wonder you rode out alone dressed like that,' he whispered.

'Hush up, old-timer.' Adams accepted his winnings from the shaking card-player who had been handling the poker-game's bank. 'Much obliged, friend.'

'I still reckon that's my money, Smith,' McGraw growled.

Gene Adams inhaled deeply.

'If those steers of yours are as good as you say they are, you'll get it all back and a lot more besides, Mr McGraw.'

The outlaw leader rubbed his chin and ambled around the table towards the rancher.

'I like ya style, Smith.'

'When can we see the cattle?' Adams asked.

McGraw glanced at his men, remembering that the brands had not been altered on the latest additions to their herd of white-faced steers.

'Tomorrow afternoon?'

'Why not now?' Adams had noticed the brands on some of the steers when he had ridden past them on his way to Cheyenne Creek. 'Me and my men are not doing anything for the rest of the day.'

'But we have to do a few things first, Smith,' McGraw said sheepishly.

'We want to settle this deal now,' Adams insisted. 'I have other herds to see besides yours. I can't waste too much time in this town.'

The outlaw leader's mind raced. He knew if he and his men worked all night they might be able to alter the brands on most of the herd by morning.

'What about tomorrow morning?'

Adams glanced at Johnny and Tomahawk, then returned his attention to One-Eyed Jake.

'OK. That'll be fine.'

'We gonna stay here all night?' Tomahawk asked Adams.

'Why not?'

Tomahawk swallowed hard. 'But this town's full of outlaws, Gene.'

Adams patted the old man's shoulder and placed a couple of coins in his wrinkled hand.

'I noticed that. Here, ask the bartender if he has a room with three cots in it.'

One-Eyed Jake McGraw looked at Adams.

'Can we take our guns with us?'

'Sure you can,' Adams agreed. 'Empty the bullets out of those guns and hand them back to our friends, Johnny.'

'You bet.' Johnny smiled.

'You're a smart man, Mr Smith.' McGraw snorted.

'That's why I've lived so long, Mr McGraw.' Adams smiled.

★   ★   ★

One-Eyed Jake McGraw and his gang had only just left the saloon when the bartender came up to Adams holding a room key in his shaking hand.

'I never seen anything like it, stranger.' The bartender sighed heavily. 'I thought you was a gonner more than a dozen times during the last ten minutes.'

Adams smiled and watched as the disgruntled crowd began to disperse. They had wanted to see a bloodbath and had been denied.

'I don't want the key, friend,' Adams said bluntly. 'We ain't staying here.'

'But I heard ya telling McGraw,' the confused man said, 'And the old critter just paid for the room.'

Tomahawk ambled up to the rancher and looked at Adams with a strained expression on his face.

'We ain't staying here tonight?'

'Nope,' Adams answered as Johnny accepted a beer from another of the bartenders and took a long swallow. 'Hurry up and finish that beer, boy.'

'Why?' Johnny asked lowering the glass from his lips. 'I thought we were staying here tonight.'

Gene Adams shook his head.

'Get my horse and bring it around the back of the saloon.'

Johnny finished the beer and placed the glass down. He started for the swing-doors.

'And bring my saddle-bags in with you, Johnny.'

Johnny walked out into the sunshine and made his way to where the chestnut mare was still tied to the hitching-rail.

'You ain't staying here?' the bartender with the side-whiskers asked once more.

'Nope. Keep the money for the room and don't forget to tell our one-eyed friend that you think Mr Smith might not be a real cattle-buyer at all.' Adams grinned.

'You ain't a cattle-buyer?'

'No I ain't.'

'What you planning to do, Gene?' Tomahawk asked as the tall rancher started towards the back room of the Golden Goose.

'Get changed out of these clothes and into my trail gear, old-timer.' Adams replied.

Tomahawk trailed the rancher.

'And then?'

Gene Adams stopped, turned and smiled broadly. He tugged the jutting beard of the confused Tomahawk.

'Then we're going to go and rustle us some steers.'

17

Cheyenne Creek grew even busier as the sun slowly set over the wooden buildings. Most of the vermin that had taken refuge within the lawless Badlands had nothing on their minds except satisfying their basic instincts. Feeding their depraved natures with all of the available sins that could be purchased, if you had the price.

But there were seven residents of Cheyenne Creek who had work to do through the coming night.

One-Eyed Jake McGraw and his gang had to change the brands on the 200 or so white-faced steers if they were to be purchased by the Kansas cattle-buyer.

It was a task that would have daunted most honest souls, but none of the men who followed the one-eyed killer was honest.

McGraw stood in the hotel lobby

smoking a long cigar as Sol Knight came down the staircase carrying half a dozen branding irons wrapped in a tattered and scorched piece of sacking. Each of the long irons had been designed to alter all the registered brands and make them appear to be Triple X markings.

Jake McGraw adjusted the eye-patch that concealed the gruesome cavity in his face until it covered the hole which had once held an eyeball. He turned and looked out through the open doorway at Quinn and Hart returning from the livery stables with seven fresh mounts.

'Zane and Jess are coming with the horses, boys.'

'About time,' Knight complained as he struggled with the heavy branding-irons.

McGraw whistled to Davis, Jones and Barnes who were dozing on a long couch near a window.

'Wake up, ya lazy sidewinders,' McGraw growled. He dropped his cigar on to the carpet and crushed it underfoot. 'We got us a lot of work to do before sun-up tomorrow if'n we're gonna fool Smith and his partners.'

Sol Knight rested against the doorframe. Sweat was pouring off his face.

'Somebody help me with these darn things. They're real heavy, y'know.'

McGraw snapped his fingers at Davis.

'Give Sol a hand with the irons, Frank.'

The yawning trio rose up off the couch, walked slowly up to the one-eyed outlaw and vainly tried to show some enthusiasm.

'Do we have to go and change them brands, Jake?' Bobby Lee Jones asked. 'Smith looks like the sort that'd buy them even if the brands show they're stolen.'

'He might be willing to buy them, but I figure his bosses up in Kansas wouldn't cotton to spending cash on rustled steers.' McGraw spat a lump of brown goo on to the carpet where his cigar butt still smouldered. He then looked up and defied the hotel clerk to say something.

The clerk knew better. He remained silent.

'I'm darn tuckered out, Jake,' Barnes confessed.

'We all are, Jeb.' One-Eyed Jake rubbed his mouth on the back of his stained sleeve. 'But just think of all that cash we'll have us by tomorrow. We'll be richer than anyone in the territory.'

The men gathered around their leader. They knew that he had been like a stick of dynamite with its fuse already lit since Smith had humiliated him in the Golden Goose earlier.

Sol Knight leaned towards McGraw and smiled.

'Where do ya figure that Smith critter has all his cattle money hid, Jake? He must have a lot of cash if'n he can buy entire herds. Right?'

McGraw nodded.

'Yeah. You got a point there, Sol. That's a darn good question. I wonder where Mr Smith does keep all that cattle money.'

'I figure he must be carrying paper money,' Frank Davis chipped in as he tried to balance the heavy branding-irons that Knight had handed him. 'If it was in five-hundred- and thousand-dollar bills, it would fit into an average wallet.'

'Davis has a point, boys.' McGraw nodded again. 'A man could carry a small fortune in paper money and nobody would even know it.'

Bobby Lee Jones adjusted his gun-belt.

'He has to have the money on him. There ain't a bank within a hundred miles of here and he knows that nobody in the Badlands would take a cheque.'

One-Eyed Jake McGraw rubbed his hands together in excitement.

'We could take that money off him and still have our herd to sell up north. That would make two paydays.'

'And Mr Smith and his two sidekicks

are sleeping in a room above the saloon.' Jones grinned. 'Or they will be a little while after that darn sun sets.'

'But he's a darn cool customer,' Knight said. He walked to the the open doorway and stared at the red sky. 'Killing him won't be easy.'

McGraw walked around Sol Knight thoughtfully.

'But it would be worth it to take that smile off his face. Smith deserves to die.'

Jess Hart dismounted, handed his reins to Quinn and ran up the wooden steps into the hotel.

'What's keeping you boys? We got the fresh mounts like you said, Jake.'

McGraw walked out on to the boardwalk and rested his knuckles on his hips. Smith had made him look like a fool in the saloon and that still riled him. The thought of stealing the cattle money from the elegant man appealed to him. Killing Smith slowly appealed to him even more.

'I don't think we'll have to do no

branding tonight,' he muttered.

Zane Quinn turned in his saddle and looked at the figure running towards them waving his arms. It was the bartender with the side-whiskers.

'Hey, Jake. Ain't that the old barkeep from the Golden Goose headin' here?' Quinn called out to his leader.

McGraw looked out over the head of the mounted Quinn. 'It sure is, Zane. He looks like a man with troubles.'

'He sure looks scared about something.'

'Yeah,' One-Eyed Jake agreed as he walked down the steps and towards the gasping bartender.

'Mr McGraw! Mr McGraw!' the bartender repeatedly called out until he reached the grim-faced outlaw.

'What is it?'

'That Smith critter ain't no cattle-buyer at all,' the bartender gasped. He was bent double and desperately trying to catch his breath.

McGraw grabbed the man by the shoulders and pulled him upright.

'He ain't?'

The bartender exhaled loudly and then continued: 'No, he ain't. I heard him talkin' to them pals of his. He ain't got no intention of buying your cattle.'

'If Smith ain't a cattle-buyer, what is he?' McGraw shook the bartender hard.

'He's a rustler.'

McGraw released his grip.

'What?'

The bartender nodded.

'I swear that I'm tellin' the truth, Mr McGraw. They've gone to steal your herd right now. I came to warn ya as quick as I could. Did I do right?'

McGraw patted the breathless man's face and staggered towards the line of horses being held in check by Zane Quinn.

'Yeah, you did good, barkeep,' the outlaw muttered.

'What's going on, Jake?' Bobby Lee Jones asked from the boardwalk.

'Smith and them two friends of his are going to steal our herd, boys,' Quinn shouted to the rest of the gang.

162

'I heard the barkeep tell Jake.'

One-Eyed Jake McGraw grabbed the mane of the nearest horse and mounted quickly. He gathered up the reins and spat at the ground again. His face was growing redder with every beat of his pounding heart.

'Smith ain't nothing more than a darn rustler just like us,' he screamed. 'Now I'm angry. Real angry. I'm gonna cut that critter into little bits and feed him to the buzzards.'

The rest of the gang stood staring in disbelief at One-Eyed Jake McGraw. They had never seen him looking so insanely furious before.

'C'mon, you sidewinders,' McGraw screamed. 'We ain't got a second to lose.'

The five other outlaws ran down the hotel steps and grabbed at the horses' bridles. They quickly mounted and waited for their brooding leader to regain control of his temper.

'We got us some cattle-thieves to catch and kill,' McGraw yelled, driving his spurs into his horse's flesh.

The seven horsemen galloped out of Cheyenne Creek towards the herd they had left a few miles west.

18

Ranchers Tom Smith, Chuck Morris and Brock Carter led a handful of their best cowhands across the northern range towards the blazing campfire. Almost every one of Gene Adams's Bar 10 cowboys were gathered around the flames that licked into the night sky.

Rip Calloway rose from the warm fire and stared out into the darkness at the approaching horsemen.

'Looks like Morris and the rest of the ranchers, boys,' the tall wrangler said.

Happy Summers had just finished a plate of beans as he sat on his saddle. In the darkness the flickering light from their fire illuminated the eight riders.

'About time they showed,' Happy said. He rose to his feet and handed his tin plate to another of their men. 'If'n they'd helped the other night, maybe we wouldn't have lost so many of our boys.'

Larry Drake shrugged as he sipped at his coffee.

'Don't go blaming them, Happy. They didn't even know that Gene had sent us up here.'

The rotund cowboy knew Larry was right. The trouble was that he felt as if he needed someone to blame for the loss of his friends.

'Reckon ya right, Larry,' Happy conceded.

The eight riders drew up beside the camp-fire and dismounted.

'What you boys doing up here on the range?' Brock Carter asked, accepting a warming cup of coffee from one of the Bar 10 men.

'Gene, Tomahawk and Johnny have gone into the Badlands after them rustlers,' Happy replied.

'But why?' Tom Smith asked.

'Maybe they figured it was the right thing to do, Tom,' Rip said coldly as he strode around the dozens of seated cowboys finishing their supper.

'I don't understand,' Morris confessed. 'What's this gotta do with them?'

Happy moved closer to the three ranchers and their ranch hands. He raised a gloved finger and pointed at each of them in turn.

'Don't ya know what happened here a couple of nights back?'

Smith's face looked strained in the light of the fire's dancing flames.

'We all noticed that we lost a couple of hundred steers between us yesterday.'

'Is that what ya mean, Happy?' Brock Carter asked.

'That's part of it.' Happy sighed. 'Sheriff Doyle came up here with some deputies and Gene sent half a dozen of us to help them look out for the rustlers.'

'The trouble is, it all went wrong,' Rip Calloway said shaking his head sadly. 'We were all taken by surprise and we lost three wranglers.'

The ranchers suddenly went quiet.

'Little Billy Vine was one of our dead,' Larry Drake said as he squared up to the stunned men.

Tom Smith removed his Stetson and respectfully held it across his chest.

'We knew nothing about it, boys. Our ranch houses are all more than ten miles from here. We heard shots but thought it was just the rustlers stampeding our stock across the river.'

'But why has Gene gone into the Badlands?' Carter asked innocently. 'Surely that's a job better suited to the sheriff?'

'Gene is the sheriff, Brock!'

'What? Where's that shirker Doyle?' Carter sighed. 'Gone fishing again?'

'Doyle's dead,' Happy answered.

Again the ranchers went silent. They suddenly realized that Gene Adams was risking his own life on their behalf.

Happy turned to the rest of the Bar 10 men.

'Come on, boys. We gotta spread out and listen out for anyone coming this way from across the river. Get ya saddle ropes ready in case we need them.'

'Make sure ya guns are loaded,' Rip added.

The men all got to their feet and started to kick dirt over the fire. It did not take long for the flames to be extinguished.

'Can we help?' Smith asked humbly.

Happy Summers pulled out his tobacco pouch from his shirt pocket and nodded.

'Yep. Another eight guns can't be sniffed at.'

Rip pointed at the river.

'That seems to be their favourite route in and out of the Badlands, boys. Fan out to either side of there and use the brush as cover.'

Morris checked his six-shooter carefully as he trailed the Bar 10 men towards the river.

'What about Gene and . . . '

'Reckon all we can do is wait, Chuck,' Happy said.

'And pray,' Larry added.

19

Gene Adams could have driven the massive herd of white-faced cattle back towards the Red River border-crossing more than thirty minutes earlier, when he and his two pals had first arrived, but he had not done anything except sit atop his chestnut mare staring back at the trail which led to Cheyenne Creek, waiting.

Waiting for One-Eyed Jake McGraw and his gang to arrive with their guns blazing. He knew that he must have made them angrier than they had ever been. Adams knew that simply to have driven the herd back to the northern Texas range would not have guaranteed that the outlaws would follow straight away.

They might have decided to wait until it suited them to return and rustle the steers again.

That was no good.

Adams had to make them follow and there was only one way he could do that. He was banking on the strange Jake McGraw seeing his newly acquired herd being driven back to Texas by the man who had humiliated him in the Golden Goose. If the Bar 10 rancher was right, they would want to kill him and Tomahawk and Johnny. To do that, they would have to follow.

The Bar 10 rancher was gambling once again.

The biggest gamble of his entire life.

It was one poker-game he knew that he had to win.

Would the rustlers become so insanely furious with him that they would throw caution to the wind and give chase?

They had to!

To all three Bar 10 riders, the past thirty minutes had seemed like an eternity. The ancient Tomahawk was nervous and it showed.

He rode his black gelding back and forth between Adams and Johnny

Puma, looking east in the direction of the distant town.

Adams tapped his spurs and allowed his horse to move towards the troubled older man.

'Take it easy, Tomahawk,' Adams said quietly. 'You'll spook the herd or Johnny. Or both.'

Tomahawk reined in.

'What are we waiting for, Gene? They're gonna catch us for sure if we just stay here.'

The rancher reached across and patted the worried rider's bony shoulder.

'I want McGraw to see us stealing the herd, old-timer.'

'But if that gang get close enough to see us, they'll be close enough to shoot us too. Right?'

Before Adams could reply a sound drew his attention to the moonlit trail. He swallowed hard and wrapped his reins around his gloved hands.

'They're coming, Tomahawk.'

'Here they come, Johnny!' Tomahawk

172

called out to the youngest member of the trio.

Johnny swung his pinto pony full circle.

'I see them.'

'They're coming in fast, Gene. Darn fast,' Tomahawk said grimly. 'I don't like it.'

Gene Adams tightened his grip on his reins with his left hand, then pulled one of his golden guns from his holster and raised it in the air.

'Now we get this herd running scared, old friend.'

He fired three times.

The shots panicked the massive herd of white-faced cattle. They rose as one and scattered in all directions.

Now it was time for the three cattlemen to use every ounce of their skills. Skills they had honed over the years.

Johnny held his reins in his left hand and swung his saddle rope around in his right. The pinto pony, like every Bar 10 horse, had been trained to face down longhorn steers and force them to back off. These steers were much less intimidating than their longhorned cousins.

The pony defied the white-faced cattle and made them turn away. Tomahawk and Adams made as much noise as they could to get the herd running.

Suddenly red-hot tapers sped over the three riders' heads.

The sound of the guns came a fraction of a second later.

'Them varmints are shootin' at us, Gene,' Tomahawk shouted, feeling his horse gathering pace beneath him.

'What did you expect them to do?' Adams called out.

Johnny drew level with his two friends. 'They're gaining on us.'

Another volley of shots tore through the darkness from the seven rustlers' guns. The pitiful sound of cattle being hit by the stray bullets echoed across the fertile land. The expert Bar 10 riders had their work cut out to their mounts to avoid the fallen steers.

Johnny drew one of his guns and fired up in the air to make the herd move even faster.

'These darn white-faces are too fat. They can't run as fast as our steers, Gene.'

'They'll have to,' Tomahawk screamed as more bullets cut through the air all around them. 'McGraw's catching us up!'

Adams stood in his stirrups, turned and looked over his broad shoulder at their pursuers.

They were getting closer, he thought.

20

It sounded like a hundred vicious thunderclaps to the cowboys who had been waiting on the Texan side of the wide Red River, but the night sky was totally clear.

As the noise increased the ground beneath their high-heeled boots trembled violently. For most of the cowboys who were secreted in the dense brush which filled nearly every gap between the stout well-nourished trees, it was something that they had never experienced before.

But for three of the Bar 10 cowboys it *was* something that they recognized. A nightmare which Happy, Rip and Larry had lived through before. Something that they knew would haunt them for the rest of their days.

'What is that?' one of the rannies asked.

'Earthquake?' another queried.

'What's happening?' Tom Smith asked as his entire body shook.

Brock Carter grabbed at Larry Drake's sleeve and hauled him close.

'What's goin' on, Larry?'

'It's the herd!' Rip Calloway yelled out from behind them.

'They're comin' back!' Happy added gritting his teeth on the end of his cigarette stub and moving through the nervous men towards the river's edge.

'But how?' Morris asked.

'There's only one way them steers would be headed back here, boys,' Rip drawled.

'It must be Gene!' Happy shouted. 'It has to be!'

'He must have stolen them steers back from the rustlers,' Larry piped up.

Suddenly it became obvious to every one of the waiting cowboys that it was the herd of white-faced cattle. The wailing of confused steers filled their ears. Then the sound of gunshots echoed from far across the river beyond the dark under-growth.

'I don't get it!' Brock Carter admitted.

'Move back aways,' Happy ordered the men around him. 'We don't know how wide them steers will wander when they come stampeding in through this darn brush.'

Rip Calloway drew his Colt and cocked its hammer.

'Keep them eyes peeled. This might be some kinda trick.'

Happy ran around the cowboys.

'Get to ya horses and uncoil them ropes. We'll have to get that herd under control mighty fast when they get back on Texan soil, otherwise they'll just spread out and keep running.'

The cowboys ran through the darkness to their horses and hastily mounted the skittish creatures. Each of them knew how to handle a stampede, but this felt different. There was a doubt in their craws as to who was actually driving the herd towards them, and why.

The deafening sound grew louder as the forty or more riders tried to control their mounts.

Chuck Morris raised a finger and pointed at the river as starlight danced across its fast-flowing surface.

'Look! Here they come!'

'Chuck's right, boys,' Happy shouted above the ear-splitting noise. 'I can see the white-faces breaking their way through the brush.'

Even though the riders were hardened, the sight which suddenly greeted their tired eyes frightened them. The herd of 500 steers were viciously fighting one another to reach the river first in their desperation to get away from the men who were behind them.

The herd came crashing through everything in its path. Only the stoutest of trees managed temporarily to slow the stampeding beasts in their attempts to reach sanctuary. But even the trunks of massive trees could not stop the terrified beasts for long on their quest to reach the Red River.

Every one of the white-face steers leapt into the cold water, frantic to get away from those who were behind them, spurring them on with ropes and firing pistols.

'Look at them critters swim!' Happy said as he mounted his buckskin cutting horse and waited alongside the rest of the cowboys.

The white faces of the cattle looked like ghosts bobbing up and down in the water as they made their frantic crossing.

The cowboys stood in their stirrups and waited with their ropes in their hands. It would be their job to try and control the terrified steers. A dangerous job, even for those who had done it all their working lives.

'Let 'em run on to the range, boys,' Larry called out to his fellow riders. 'We can circle the critters when they start running out of steam.'

'I bet that they'll scatter, boys,' Happy predicted as he held his buckskin in check.

Every horseman readied himself in anticipation of the cattle reaching dry land again. Sweat poured down from beneath the hatbands of their Stetsons as fear defied the cool night air.

A hundred cannons could not have made more noise.

The hundreds of steers ploughed their way up the steep slope from the river and raced out on to the Texas range. The horsemen controlled their mounts and waited until every one of the beasts had reached the high grassland.

As Happy Summers had predicted, the steers scattered in all directions.

'Go get 'em!' he ordered.

The riders spurred and urged their cutting horses across the almost level range through the swaying grass. Twirling their cutting ropes in wide circles over their heads they drove their mounts hard and soon began to overtake the flagging cattle and force them into a smaller and smaller circle.

The skilled horsemen rode wide

beneath the canopy of a myriad twinkling stars.

Happy Summers and Rip Calloway remained near the river on their horses. They had both drawn their pistols and waited with narrowed eyes, watching the opposite bank of the Red River.

Both cowboys could hear the sound of gunshots still, ringing out from the Badlands. Neither man said anything as the noise of the guns drew closer.

Then they saw the three familiar riders galloping through the brush, aiming their mounts into the river.

Happy was about to speak when he realized that their Bar 10 comrades all had their guns holstered and yet the sound of guns being fired was still echoing all around them.

Rip spurred his horse and rode to the side of Happy's buckskin gelding.

'The rustlers must be chasing them, Happy!' the anxious cowboy exclaimed.

Happy rubbed his eyes along the back of his coat sleeve and squinted into the darkness.

'Look!'

Rip stretched himself to his full height in his stirrups and looked over the heads of the three fast-approaching riders. He could see the flashes of gunfire lighting up the trail beyond the trees as the sound of shots filled their ears.

'Look, Happy. It's them darn rustlers chasing Gene and the boys.' Rip gasped.

'Get that head of yours down, Rip,' Gene Adams shouted as he rode up the muddy slope ahead of Tomahawk and Johnny.

One-Eyed Jake McGraw led his six-strong gang out of the dense brush and down into the river after the Bar 10 riders. Their guns were still blazing, seeking the backs of their fleeing prey.

Adams hauled his reins up to his chest as his mount reached the long swaying grass. He turned the mare and then watched as the seven outlaws continued to drive their mounts across the river.

'Take cover,' the rancher ordered. 'These *hombres* mean business.'

Tomahawk had almost reached the other horsemen when he felt his mount stagger beneath him. The black gelding arched and fell heavily, sending its master flying across its neck.

Johnny pulled back on his reins and then leapt from the pinto pony beside the fallen Tomahawk.

'You OK, old-timer?'

Tomahawk crawled from beside his horse and tried to see in the darkness.

'What happened to my horse, boy?'

Johnny knelt and helped Tomahawk off the ground.

'The poor critter took a bullet or two by the looks of it.'

'Ain't that just dandy? Took me two years to train that critter.' Tomahawk hauled his gun from its holster and cocked the hammer. 'I'm gonna kill them rustlin' sons of . . . '

'Now keep ya head down.' Johnny kept hold of the skinny arm and led his dazed pal to the cover of the trees.

184

With outlaw bullets raining on them, the rest of the cowboys threw themselves from their saddles and dived for cover. Gene Adams knelt and reloaded both his golden Colts in turn.

'Here they come, boys,' he yelled.

McGraw dug his spurs into his horse and led his men over the lip of the slope. Their guns blazed lethal lead down at the crouching cowboys.

Only the darkness shielded the Bar 10 men from their attackers' fury.

Rip Calloway fanned the hammer of his Colt up at the seven riders. As the cowboy saw one of his shots take Jeb Barnes off his saddle he felt a hot burning bullet tear into his flesh and knock him off his feet.

Happy picked up his saddle rope from the ground and began to swing it over his head. He released the length and floated it over the horsemen. Using his immense weight, he hauled its loop tight and watched Sol Knight and Frank Davis being dragged over the cantles of their saddles.

Gene Adams knelt and fired into the blackness at the confused riders above him. Jess Hart was hit high and then tumbled lifelessly into the long grass.

Red-hot bullets burned through the darkness in all directions as the rustlers and the cowboys continued to wage war on each other.

Johnny Puma felt the heat of an outlaw's bullet as it tore through his shirt and grazed his ribs. He dropped his guns and fell into the arms of Tomahawk.

'Are you OK, Johnny?' the old-timer screamed above the sound of the gunfire.

Johnny rolled off the older man's knees and on to the grass, clutching his bleeding side.

'Hush up, old-timer. I'm OK. Just winged.'

The acrid stench of choking gun-smoke filled the night air and blinded the men who sought to end each others' lives.

Zane Quinn was seated on his saddle

186

trying to reload his guns when bullets ripped into his back. The outlaw dropped his weaponry and grabbed his horse's mane. As he slid from his saddle towards the ground, his eyes saw Bobby Lee Jones's smoking barrels behind him.

The expression on Jones's face told the older outlaw who had ended his miserable existence. Jones spurred his horse to get closer to the man he had just killed when Rip Calloway raised his Colt and blasted.

Bobby Lee Jones felt the cowboy's bullet hit him squarely in the middle of his chest. It was like being kicked by a mule. He was lifted into the air, then he crashed under the hoofs of the stray mounts.

Suddenly the sound of gunfire came off the range. McGraw swung his horse around and looked at the guns of the forty cowboys lighting up the night sky. They were now coming to the aid of Gene Adams and his men.

Realizing that he was now alone,

One-Eyed Jake went to return to the Badlands but Happy Summers had placed himself between the outlaw and the river. The cowboy fanned his gun hammer and made the outlaw duck and turn his horse.

'Where are ya, Smith?' McGraw screamed at the top of his lungs as he hastily reloaded his guns.

Gene Adams moved through the smoke towards the outlaw. The starlight flashed across the star on his shirt.

'The name's Adams, McGraw. Sheriff Gene Adams.'

One-Eyed Jake squeezed the trigger of his gun when he saw the rancher heading straight at him. The bullet caught Adams in his left shoulder sending him falling through the dense undergrowth and sliding down towards the river.

The insane laughter of the deranged outlaw came to an abrupt halt when Johnny Puma managed to find one of his pistols in the long grass and fire at the one-eyed McGraw.

McGraw buckled backwards in his saddle as he felt his Stetson torn from his head with part of his scalp. Somehow he managed to keep hold of his gun as blood poured down his face from the deep gash.

McGraw fired at Johnny.

The gun was ripped from the hand of the young cowboy.

Then the one-eyed outlaw spurred his horse viciously again and galloped towards the distant high mesas that edged the vast range.

Tomahawk made his way to the edge of the steep slope and shouted down into the blackness.

'You OK, Gene?'

Gene Adams crawled back up from the river-bank and rested an arm on the bony shoulder of his oldest friend.

'You're bleeding, Gene,' Tomahawk gasped.

'It ain't nothing, old timer. Just a graze.' Adams sighed as he watched the forty or more cowboys reining in next to them.

'Are you OK, Gene?' Carter asked.

'I'm in better condition than these darn outlaws, Brock.'

Just then Sol Knight, lying on the spot where he had landed after being roped by Happy regained consciousness. The outlaw stared at the dozens of horsemen before recognizing the voice of the man he knew as Smith. Knight moved his right hand across his belly, pulled the grip of his pistol from its holster and carefully cocked its hammer until it was fully locked.

He rolled over on to his side and then managed to raise himself on to his knees.

'Ya gonna die, Smith!' Knight yelled as his arm rose to eye-level and he aimed the deadly gun at Gene Adams.

Tomahawk pushed the rancher aside, dragged his Indian axe from his belt and threw it with all his force at the outlaw.

The tomahawk hit Knight in the centre of his face. It was a lethal blow delivered with masterly accuracy.

'That'll teach him,' Tomahawk muttered. He walked across to the dead outlaw and plucked his hatchet off the ground.

'You saved my life, old-timer,' Adams said.

'Again, Gene. I saved ya life again,' Tomahawk answered wiping the blood off the honed blade before returning it to his belt.

'Where's McGraw?' Adams asked.

'He rode off towards the mountains, Gene,' Johnny replied, nursing his wounds.

The Bar 10 rancher did not say anything. He made his way past the mounted men until he reached his chestnut mare.

'Where we going, Gene?' Tomahawk asked.

Adams held on to the saddle horn, then put his left boot into the stirrup and mounted the tall animal. He gathered up his reins and allowed the horse to walk to the cowboys.

'I'm going after that one-eyed maniac alone.'

'What?' Tomahawk gasped.

'You boys stay here and get that herd settled,' Adams ordered. He turned the head of the mare. 'I'm the sheriff and I'm gonna get that varmint. Dead or alive, I'm gonna get him.'

The horsemen watched as Gene Adams spurred his horse and galloped across the grassland. Within seconds he had disappeared into the shadows of night.

★　★　★

For hours the chestnut mare trailed the outlaw through the tall swaying grass. Then as the sun began to light up the sky above them, McGraw turned and fired at his relentless pursuer.

Gene Adams returned fire and continued to chase his fleeing prey. With every stride of their horses they drew closer and closer to the high mountain ranges. Adams urged his mare to gain pace when he saw that McGraw was getting near the rocky outcrop.

The rancher knew this land well. Once a man reached the high trails he could pick off anyone on the grassy range below him.

The mesas rose heavenward like giants.

The outlaw turned in his saddle again and fired. The bullet took the black ten-gallon hat off Adams's head. The rancher raised his right-hand golden Colt and fired.

This time the deadly bullet found a target.

McGraw went head over heels when his wounded mount fell heavily beneath him. The bruised and bleeding outlaw staggered to his feet and watched as the chestnut mare thundered towards him.

He fired again, then turned on his heels and ran towards the wall of solid rock which seemed to rise until it touched the very roof of the sky itself.

One-Eyed Jake McGraw desperately started to climb.

The rancher stopped his horse and leapt from his saddle to a high rocky ledge. He checked his guns, then started to follow the outlaw up the side of the mountain.

Every few yards McGraw fired down at the man wearing the sheriff's star on his shirt. Adams returned fire and continued to chase the outlaw further up the side of the mountain.

For more than ten minutes the men continued their dangerous ascent. Then the outlaw reached the flat summit and used the last of his bullets in a vain attempt to kill the man who simply refused to stop his chase.

Adams rested against a dew-covered rock wall and tried to catch his breath. He checked his guns again and holstered one before edging his way higher.

Jake McGraw looked down on the defiant rancher and smiled. Now he could simply wait until there was no cover for Adams to hide behind. He emptied his spent cartridge shells from his Colt, then fumbled around his gunbelt for bullets.

The one-eyed outlaw could not find any.

He quickly unbuckled the belt and stared along the cartridge pockets for bullets.

There was none left.

And Adams was getting closer and closer to the flat-topped mountain summit.

Now it was his turn to bluff, McGraw thought. He held the empty gun in his hand and aimed it down at Adams.

'Ya better turn around and get going.'

Adams stopped again and peered up at the outlaw waving his gun at him.

'Why don't you shoot, McGraw?'

'I'm being generous. You get going and I'll let ya live.'

Gene Adams slid his Colt into its holster and stood away from the rockface. He looked up at the outlaw and smiled.

'There ain't a generous bone in your rancid body, McGraw.'

The outlaw kept his empty gun

aimed at the rancher.

'What ya doing? Quit smilin'.'

'You're out of shells, ain't you?' Adams started to walk up the perilous slope towards the snarling outlaw. 'Go on, McGraw. Prove me wrong and shoot me.'

Jake McGraw stood and took slow steps backwards as Adams got closer and closer.

Both men stood on the top of the flat mountain summit, staring at one another.

'I'm gonna have to kill you, Smith. Or whatever ya real name is,' McGraw snarled. He walked towards the man wearing the gleaming star on his chest.

'Not with that gun, you ain't.' Adams smiled.

McGraw screamed insanely and threw the empty gun at Adams. The rancher ducked and heard it bouncing down the side of the mountain.

'You've done laughed once too often at me.'

Adams shrugged.

'Reckon?'

The outlaw seemed suddenly to go silent. His chin dropped and his mouth opened. Drool dripped from the quivering lower lip the closer the outlaw got to the rancher.

Adams had faced many things in his time, but never a man who seemed so crazed before. He wanted to draw and shoot this creature for what he had done. Yet Gene Adams could not go against a lifetime of morality and shoot an unarmed man. However depraved that man was.

The rancher unbuckled his gunbelt and allowed it to fall behind him. He raised his gloved fists and stepped forward.

'Reckon I might regret this, McGraw.'

Both men threw themselves towards one another. The outlaw smashed a left and a right into Adams's body before the Bar 10 man managed to throw a hefty right-cross on to the chin of the crazed outlaw.

McGraw fell on to his side and rolled

over and over. He could see the rancher running towards him. The one-eyed man grabbed Adam's legs and pulled with all his might.

Adams fell.

As the rancher hit the hard ground, he heard the outlaw moving behind him. He twisted on the ground until he was on one knee. Too late, he saw the boot.

McGraw kicked Adams under his chin and sent the older man flying backwards toward the edge of the sheer drop.

Adams grabbed at a rock and stopped himself from plummeting off the high mountain-top. He glanced down and then scrambled to his feet. The outlaw smiled and moved closer again.

Then Adams realized why he was smiling.

The morning sun glinted off the edge of the deadly knife he had pulled from his boot.

'I'm gonna gut ya like a fish.'

Adams walked to his side. With every step he stared at the knife's lethal blade. He glanced at his guns in their holsters lying on the ground but he could not reach them. McGraw had managed to get himself between the rancher and the gunbelt.

'You any good with that toothpick?' Adams asked, his mind racing.

'Good enough to have killed more than twenty men like you over the years,' One-Eyed Jake replied. He started to narrow the distance between them.

Gene Adams had just stepped backwards when the heel of his left boot felt the edge of the cliff. He swallowed hard. He could do nothing but watch as the smiling man kept coming towards him, waving the knife.

'I reckon I made a darn big mistake coming after you alone, McGraw,' Adams said, glancing over his shoulder at the terrifying drop.

The outlaw stopped for a moment.

'You sure are the coolest customer

I've ever met, Mr Smith.'

Adams lowered his head and then suddenly charged at the outlaw. The blade flashed and the rancher felt a pain in his arm as he hit McGraw off his feet.

The razor-harp knife had slid across the entire length of Adams's left arm. Blood trailed down the wound and filled his glove.

McGraw rolled over and began to rise. Adams kicked the deadly knife out of the outlaw's hand. It slid towards the edge of the cliff.

The outlaw jumped to his feet and tried to reach it. But Adams grabbed the outlaw and smashed a clenched right uppercut to Jake McGraw's jaw.

The powerful punch sent the one-eyed man crashing across the hard ground. He rolled over and over. As McGraw's body came to a halt, he reached out for the knife again.

Adams knew that the outlaw was too close to the edge of the cliff for him to try and stop him again. He looked over his shoulder and ran for his gunbelt.

As the rancher scooped the belt off the ground and pulled one of his golden pistols from its holster he saw McGraw rise to his feet with the knife in his hand.

Jake McGraw leaned back, raised the knife and went to throw it at the Bar 10 man. Adams dragged the hammer back on his Colt and fired at the outlaw's lethal weapon.

The bullet hit the long gleaming blade and sent it falling down to the range below. Before Adams could do anything he watched in horror as the crazed outlaw turned and stared at his knife disappearing into the morning mist that was rising off the range as the sun warmed its surface.

It was as if Jake McGraw was trying to follow his knife without any awareness of the consequences.

As Gene Adams stood on the edge of the cliff he wondered why McGraw would have done such a thing. The rancher had no knowledge of the twisted mind that had grown to revere the knife that had enabled him to escape the Boston Asylum for the Insane.

Finale

Gene Adams stood beside Tomahawk amid the sea of bluebonnets that seemed to go on for ever. This was where they buried their dead on the Bar 10. It had become a holy place where the tall rancher never allowed any of his precious longhorn steers to graze. This was the way it had always been. The same as when he and Tomahawk had first set eyes upon it. This was where they had buried the dead from the wagon train all those years earlier. This had been the beginning of the Bar 10, the reason Gene Adams could never leave this land. Amy was buried here. Over the years he had laid his Bar 10 cowboys to rest beneath the carpet of beautiful flowers.

Billy Vine, Don Cooper and Josh Weaver had joined their Bar 10 friends here. But the wild flowers spread quickly and covered all signs of their graves.

'We ought to put some headstones here, Gene,' Tomahawk suggested.

'I never liked headstones, old-timer.' Adams sighed as they turned and started to walk towards their waiting horses.

'Why not, boy?'

'I always reckoned that if your name is on a marker stone, you're stuck. Could stop them getting to wherever they're headed,' Adams said thoughtfully.

Tomahawk mounted his new horse and nodded.

'That's somethin' to think about.'

The rancher looked up at his oldest friend. 'Can you remember where we buried Amy, Tomahawk?'

The ancient eyes surveyed the ocean of flowers before he rubbed his beard and pointed to where Adams's horse was standing quietly stroking the ground with its hoof.

'I'm darn sure that it was somewhere

around where ya mare is standing right now, Gene. Why?'

'No reason, old-timer.' Adams smiled.

Tomahawk looked at his horse and shrugged.

'This horse ain't no smarter than my last one, Gene. Couldn't find snow in a blizzard.'

Adams patted the horse.

'Just like its master.'

'Yep. Well I'm headed back. I can smell supper cooking.' Tomahawk laughed.

Gene Adams watched as the older man tapped his spurs into the side of the young horse and rode off towards the distant ranch house.

The rancher looked at his tall chestnut mare.

'Given any thought to me giving you a name, girl?'

The mare nodded and snorted as her master picked up the loose reins and looped them over her head. He smiled and then mounted.

'What about me calling you Amy?'

The horse nodded again.

Gene Adams ran a gloved hand down the neck of the handsome horse and then looked out at the blue flowers. He felt a lump in his throat and turned the horse.

'Come on, Amy. Let's go home.'

We do hope that you have enjoyed reading this large print book.

Did you know that all of our titles are available for purchase?

We publish a wide range of high quality large print books including:
**Romances, Mysteries, Classics
General Fiction
Non Fiction and Westerns**

Special interest titles available in large print are:
**The Little Oxford Dictionary
Music Book, Song Book
Hymn Book, Service Book**

Also available from us courtesy of Oxford University Press:
**Young Readers' Dictionary
(large print edition)
Young Readers' Thesaurus
(large print edition)**

For further information or a free brochure, please contact us at:
**Ulverscroft Large Print Books Ltd.,
The Green, Bradgate Road, Anstey,
Leicester, LE7 7FU, England.
Tel:** (00 44) 0116 236 4325
Fax: (00 44) 0116 234 0205

COLD GUNS

Caleb Rand

A few years after the Civil War, Lou Hollister returns to Texas, bearing the cruel scars of an enemy prison stockade. Once home, he thinks he can settle and cast off a beleaguered past. Instead, he finds a family without hope, and a ranch manipulated by Tusk Tollinger, the corrupt sheriff of Cottonwood County. Lou fights to regain his ranch, and when a great snowstorm surges in from the Sacramento Mountains, he must confront his tormentors from the past. Can he now wreak his final, bloody revenge?